Dear Reader,

I wrote *Baby Makes Three* because families
fascinate me, and I don't think you have to be
related by blood to consider yourself "family."
I wanted to explore the dynamics of a single
father who was raising a child that wasn't his,
but because of his profound sense of family, did
the only thing he could—accepted this child and
raised and claimed it as his own. It's one thing to
claim you're a father, but it's quite another to live
it—to put a child's needs first before your own.
Not many men could do that for a child that
wasn't even theirs, but "Wild Bill" Cody did,
even though he knew that it would cost him his
career. Men continually surprise me—pleasantly—
"Wild Bill" Cody, the hero and single "father" in
this story turned out to be a wonderful man and
a truly terrific father. I fell in love with him, and
hope you will, too.

Sharon De Vita

SHARON DE VITA

is a *USA Today* bestselling, award-winning author of over twenty-four books of fiction and nonfiction, including one that's been optioned as an NBC *Movie of the Week*. A former Adjunct Professor of Literature and Communication, Sharon's first book won a national writing competition for Best Unpublished Romance Novel of 1985. This award-winning book, *Heavenly Match*, was subsequently published by Silhouette. With almost 2 million copies of her Silhouette books in print and translations in 13 languages, Sharon's professional credentials have earned her a place in *Who's Who in American Authors, Editors and Poets* as well as in the *International Who's Who of Authors*. In 1987, Sharon was the proud recipient of *Romantic Times Magazine's* Lifetime Achievement Award for Excellence in Writing. A newlywed, Sharon and her husband, a retired U.S. colonel, have seven grown children between them and currently reside in Arizona.

Books by Sharon De Vita

babies
& BACHELORS USA

Sharon De Vita
Baby Makes Three

Published by Silhouette Books

America's Publisher of Contemporary Romance

Once in a while, you meet someone who touches your life, and changes it.

This book is dedicated to three such people
who have touched my life, and changed it.

Karen Solem	Tara Hughes	Alice Alfonsi
Editor-in-Chief	Senior Editor	Assistant Editor
Silhouette Books	Silhouette Books	Silhouette Books

Thank you all...for taking a chance...
...and giving me a chance.

SILHOUETTE BOOKS

ISBN 0-373-82297-9

BABY MAKES THREE

This edition published by arrangement with Harlequin Books S.A.

® and TM are trademarks of Harlequin Books S.A., used under license.
Trademarks indicated with ® are registered in the United States Patent
and Trademark Office, the Canadian Trade Marks Office and in other
countries.

Visit Silhouette at www.eHarlequin.com

Printed in U.S.A.

Chapter One

"**D**arling, put your pants back on."

Darling put your pants back on? Frowning, Maggy drew back and looked at the telephone receiver strangely. "Mother, is there someone there with you?"

"Well, dear… I guess you could say I have company."

"Company?" Maggy said slowly. "What *kind* of company?"

"Why dear, male company, of course."

"Do you mean to tell me," Maggy croaked, "that you have a male in the house *without his pants on*?"

"To tell you the truth, dear," her mother admitted with a soft chuckle, "he really doesn't have much of *anything* on."

Maggy held the phone aside so she could swear.

"What on earth is this person doing in your house without his pants on? Never mind, Mother," she went on, shaking her head. "I'm not sure I want to know. May I ask how on earth you met this... person?"

"Actually, I just met Bobby today. And Maggy, he has the most glorious blue eyes," her mother gushed. "Wait until you meet him."

Aware that her boss Miss Barklay was sitting in the next office, Maggy cupped her hand over the receiver. "Do you mean to tell me that you let a perfect stranger in your house *because you liked his eyes*!"

"Don't be ridiculous, dear," her mother chided. "I liked much more than his eyes. He also has a wonderful smile. Although it would be much nicer if he had all his teeth."

"Had all his *what*!" Maggy cried, bouncing out of her chair.

"*Teeth*, dear," her mother repeated sweetly as Maggy began to pace frantically around her office.

"Mother...mmm...what...does this...person do for a living?"

"Do?" Elizabeth hesitated. "Well dear, Bobby really doesn't *do* anything. He has very simple needs, though," she added cheerfully. "A bottle now and then and he's really quite happy."

"Oh Lord!" Maggy moaned, almost dropping the receiver as visions of a toothless wino danced through her mind. "Mother, now listen very carefully to me. I'm on my way home. I want you to—"

"Got to run now, dear. Bobby's waiting. I'm going to take him to lunch."

"You're taking him? Mother! *Mother!*"

Elizabeth plunked down the receiver. Chuckling softly, she bent down to scoop up two-year-old Bobby off the floor.

"Shame on you, Elizabeth," the man on her couch scolded, wagging a finger at her.

Mindful of the posted speed limit, Maggy roared through the streets. There had to be a logical reason why her mother was entertaining a naked man in the middle of the afternoon. On the other hand, she thought with a frown, whatever her mother was involved in generally bore no resemblance to logic or reason. Elizabeth had done some wild things in her days, but this time she had gone too far.

Consorting with a toothless derelict of questionable character who had a fondness for the bottle and Lord knows what other decadent pleasures was going too far, even for *her* mother.

It was a good thing most of her mother's money was invested in good blue-chip stocks and T-bills; otherwise her crazy assortment of friends would surely have run through it by now.

There was no way some slick-talking gigolo could get his hands on her mother's money, Maggy thought confidently. At least not without her knowing about it. A sudden thought caused her hands to tighten on the steering wheel. There *was* her mother's monthly allowance. Not a fortune for sure, but certainly enough to keep some wine-guzzling pervert in fine style.

Pulling into the long, climbing driveway of her mother's estate, Maggy slammed on her brakes and brought her Mercedes to a screeching halt. Snatching her briefcase off the seat, she shot out of the car and hurried up the walk. She had absolutely no idea what her mother had gotten herself into this time, but she fully intended to put a stop to it. Now, before her mother got hurt.

"Well, I'll be…" Cody muttered. His deep Tennessee voice lilted with humor as he peered through the curtains at the young woman storming up the walk. From Elizabeth's description of her daughter, he'd thought for sure she'd be a sourpuss of a matron whose idea of a good time was walking neutered poodles. But this woman… His twinkling blue eyes quickly ran the length of her. Although diminutive in stature, she carried herself with regal bearing. Her cool blond hair fell in glossy, layered waves to her shoulders. He couldn't tell the color of her eyes from this distance, but he could see enough of her to know she was breathtakingly beautiful.

"She's home," Elizabeth whispered gleefully, trying to peek over Cody's broad shoulder. Catching the determined look on her daughter's face, she sighed heavily. "Oh Cody, I don't know what's come over that girl lately. I think that finishing school she works at has finished her off. I tell you, she's much too serious for her own good." Elizabeth clucked her tongue in dismay. "Cody, she doesn't have an ounce of fun in her."

Cody's eyes went to the young woman again and he nodded. She was impeccably dressed, if one was an undertaker. Even in the blistering heat of the August day, her expensively tailored clothing didn't have a wrinkle in it. The suit fitted her slender body well, giving just the barest hint of the curves that lay beneath. The only touch of femininity was a colorful scarf that was tied primly at her throat. Her long legs were shapely, her tiny feet encased in a pair of black pumps that looked shiny enough to see one's reflection in them. Her clothing quietly but firmly insisted that this was a woman who took life seriously, thought Cody. She probably planned out each and every idea, motion and movement, leaving nothing to chance or fate—poor thing.

"Well, Elizabeth," Cody drawled, letting his lips curve into a mischievous smile. "Why don't *we* see if we can put some fun in her life?"

Elizabeth smiled with relief. "Maggy's really a wonderful woman, Cody," she explained hurriedly. "She really can't do much about being—stuffy. It's that job of hers. I'm sure Maggy will help you." She patted his broad arm. "Wait and see," Elizabeth said with false cheer. "She'll grow on you."

Warts could grow on you, Cody decided. Margaret Magee, however, he wasn't quite so sure of. Yet despite her austere appearance there was something about the woman, a hint of vulnerability that made him curious. What was hiding beneath the prim clothes and serious demeanor? Cody didn't know, but he had a feeling he was going to have a hell of a lot of fun finding out.

"Why don't you let me handle her?" he suggested, and Elizabeth nodded as she headed toward the door.

"Maggy darling!" Smiling, Elizabeth opened the door with a flourish. "What a surprise! I didn't expect you home so early."

Blinking rapidly, Maggy swallowed a smile. Her mother's clothing always was a shock to her visual senses, but today she seemed to have outdone herself. A silk something or other in a violent shade of purple flowed and billowed from her slender frame. Her feet were clad in enormously high-heeled sandals that caused her to totter precariously. A red and green plaid bow was gaily tied around her silver head, giving her the appearance of a slightly wilting Christmas decoration.

Deciding to ignore her mother's outlandish appearance—at least for the moment—Maggy bent to kiss her cheek. "Where is he, Mother?"

"Where's who?"

"Your friend...Bobby?"

"He's taking a nap, dear." Elizabeth shut the door.

"He's *what*?" Maggy looked at her mother in disbelief, totally unaware of Cody's scrutiny. From his vantage point in the living room he could see yet not be seen, which suited him fine for the moment.

"Darling, he's tired. Bobby's had quite a bit of exercise this morning. He has so much energy, dear." Her mother sighed dreamily. "Since your father died, I've not been used to so much…physical activity."

Maggy felt her cheeks go pink at her mother's words. Shaking her head, she dropped an arm affectionately around her mother's shoulder. "I realize that you've been lonely since Father died. But certainly it's not necessary for you to—" Maggy stopped abruptly as she searched for the correct word "—to cavort with men of unscrupulous character," she finished softly, causing Cody to chuckle. The deep-throated laughter was definitely masculine, and Maggy whirled in the direction of the sound.

Her eyes widened and her mouth fell open in shock as her gaze collided with the deepest, bluest eyes she'd ever seen. For a moment, her breath crawled back down her throat. Her mother certainly had been right about one thing; he *did* have glorious eyes.

Stunned, Maggy allowed her gaze to scan the rest of him. Tall and rugged, there was something faintly

primitive about the man. While his hair was as dark
and silky as a raven's wing, it was much too long
for her tastes, but it matched the rest of his appearance quite naturally.

His face was nothing short of stunning, comprised
of sharp planes and angles that fit together like the
jagged edges of a jigsaw puzzle. His mouth was full
and sensuous, his chin square and proud, with just
the slightest hint of a cleft.

Male strength and rugged masculinity seemed to
throb from every inch of him; from the deeply
scarred boots that covered his feet, the faded cham-
bray shirt that stretched wide across his broad shoulders, to the comfortable well-worn jeans that hugged
his frame in all the right masculine places.

"Like what you see?" Cody teased, his eyes
alight with sudden mischief. At his words, Maggy's
jaw clicked shut.

A crooked grin tilted his mouth and his blue eyes
prowled over her, perusing her in the same slow,
painstaking way that she had just studied him. For
some reason, Maggy had a sudden urge to turn and
flee. Hungry eyes, she thought dully. He was the
kind of man she'd always avoided. The kind of man
who was as secure of himself and his masculinity
as she was insecure.

Drawing herself up, Maggy attempted to glare at
him, to give him the look that usually caused the
students at Miss Avalon's to freeze in fear, but it
obviously had no such effect on this man. He bla-

tantly stared right back until she was forced to look away.

She was not used to being unsettled by anyone, least of all by a man. But *this* man apparently enjoyed breaking all the rules of polite society. His mere presence was evidence of that. While her personal experience with men was practically nil, in her position as assistant headmistress of Miss Avalon's Academy for Young Ladies, Maggy had, on occasion, dealt with all kinds of men. But there was something decidedly different about this man, something that was somehow scrambling her nerves.

Fighting her own feminine response, Maggy wondered again what he was doing in *her house with her mother*. Women probably flocked around him like birds around breadcrumbs, she thought dully. No wonder her poor mother had let him in the house!

"Mother, I thought you said he was taking a nap?" She couldn't prevent the hint of censure that colored her words.

"*Bobby*'s taking a nap," Elizabeth qualified, only causing her daughter more confusion.

"If Bobby's taking a nap," Maggy said carefully, acutely aware that the man's blue eyes were still meandering over her, "who on earth is *this*?"

"*This* is Cody," Elizabeth announced, turning to trot into the living room. "Come along, Maggy dear, you're looking a little peaked. Some tea might perk you up."

"I don't want any tea, Mother," Maggy said tightly, dragging her eyes from Cody's as she followed her mother. "And I don't want to be perked up. What I want is to know what's going on. Who is this man?" she hissed, deliberately ignoring Cody, who was just behind her. She had the uncanny feeling the man was now checking out her backside, but wasn't about to turn around to find out, fearing she was right.

"The name's Bill Cody," he drawled, his accent more pronounced as it curled softly around his words. "*Wild Bill* Cody."

Maggy's lips pursed in displeasure. *Wild Bill* indeed! Somehow it didn't surprise her. From the looks of this man she could just imagine how he had earned his nickname, and it probably wasn't for his dancing.

"My friends call me Cody," he went on pleasantly, leaning one broad shoulder against the wall and letting his gaze travel over her again.

The look in his eyes was warm enough to scorch the starch in her blouse, and Maggy drew herself up, trying not to let on how much this man and those eyes were affecting her.

"I shall call you *Mr.* Cody," she returned coolly. "Until something more…appropriate occurs to me."

"Honey, from the look on your face," he teased, "I've got a feeling something…more appropriate has already occurred to you."

At his words Maggy's mouth slammed shut once again and her briefcase fell from her nerveless fingers, landing on the oak floor with a resounding thud. There was no point in standing here trading verbal insults with the man. She'd find out exactly what was going on, and *then* she'd throw him out! Giving him a scathing look, Maggy turned toward her mother.

"What is going on here?" she demanded.

"There's no reason to get upset, dear." Elizabeth cast a worried look at her daughter. "Cody and Bobby need our help."

Wonderful, Maggy groaned inwardly. Naked Bobby was taking a nap and Lord knows what this man thought he was doing. She turned to study him cautiously, wondering just what kind of scam he was trying to pull. Whatever it was, it wasn't going to work. She could just imagine the kind of help he needed. No doubt it was cash, probably just enough to tide them over, she thought darkly.

"And you told him *we*'d help him?" Maggy asked, her voice incredulous.

"Well of course, dear," Elizabeth admitted, flashing Cody an affectionate smile. Maggy whirled on him, and he had the audacity to wink at her! Fury darkened her emerald eyes.

"Mr. Cody," she said tightly. "May I see you privately for a moment?"

It wasn't a question, but a command, Cody noted as he pulled himself upright, prepared to follow her.

"We'll be back in a moment, Mother." Maggy turned on her heel and marched into the kitchen. Abruptly she turned to face the man looming behind her. He was standing so close, she would've been nose-to-nose with him, if he hadn't been so tall. As it was, she was nose-to-chest with him, and it threw her off balance for just a moment—long enough for that wicked grin to claim his mouth again.

Squaring her shoulders, Maggy inhaled deeply in an effort to compose herself. It was best to handle these things quickly and directly. The sooner she found out what he wanted, or rather *how much* he wanted, the sooner she could get rid of him. And, she thought darkly, it wouldn't be a moment too soon!

"All right, Mr. Cody," she said quietly, tilting her head back and forcing herself to meet those eyes. "How much?" Her voice vibrated with suppressed rage, and he frowned down at her.

"How much what?"

"How much do you want to leave my mother alone?"

"To leave your mother alone?" He threw his head back and roared, much to her annoyance. "You think I'm after your mother's money?" he asked incredulously.

"Come on now, do you really think you're the first person to play on my mother's sympathies? My mother's an easy touch. She's a rich, lonely widow with a soft heart and a kind soul. And she's just a bit naive. But *I*'m not,'' Maggy added deliberately, putting as much frost into her words as possible.

"*Naive* wasn't quite the word I was thinking of calling you,'' Cody admitted softly. His voice was low and deliberately seductive. He was so close Maggy could smell the subtle hint of his cologne; she could almost feel his body heat. Her nerves fluttered with a flurry of sensations as pure feminine panic clutched at her heart.

"How much?'' she finally managed to stammer again.

"You know,'' Cody said, leaning closer to inspect her and shaking his head sadly. "I'm having a hard time believing you're really Elizabeth's daughter. She's so full of life and spirit. But you, honey, don't look like you've got an ounce of life in you. In fact, if I were you, I'd be careful not to lie down. Someone might start throwing dirt on top of you!''

Maggy's jaw dropped open as if it had come unhinged and she inhaled a great gust of air through her nose. "I don't think this is very funny!''

"Maybe that's your problem,'' he teased, his eyes dancing with mischief. "I've got a feeling you don't think anything's funny.''

"I'm a very busy woman, Mr. Cody, and I don't have time to be fooling around with you. Just tell me what you want.''

"I guarantee that what we're doing right now is *not* fooling around,'' Cody murmured, leaning close to her until his breath ruffled her hair. "If we were fooling around, believe me, you'd know it."

Unexpectedly, Cody reached up to brush a wisp of hair from her cheek and her knees went weak as awareness skipped across her nerve endings like pebbles across a lake. Her breath stalled, and Maggy could see her own stricken expression reflected in the depths of his eyes.

Sucking in air in an effort to release the constriction in her chest, Maggy found herself suddenly light-headed. She was flustered, and totally off balance. But what was worse, he knew it.

And, she thought furiously, he had the bad manners to be enjoying her distress! She tried to take another step back to distance herself from him, but her feet weren't getting the message her mind was sending.

"Don't worry," Cody said cheerfully. "I'm not in the least bit interested in your mother's money. The only thing I want from you is a little courtesy." His eyes twinkled and he gave her cheek a quick little pat. "*If* you can manage it?"

She wasn't certain what angered her more, the fact that he had the audacity to touch her or that he had done it in such a patronizing way. "Look," Maggy snapped, her eyes blazing, "I'm tired of—"

A sudden wail from the other room cut off her words. Cody ducked around her and through the door just as Elizabeth entered the living room—with a wailing child tucked securely under her arm. The toddler took one look at Maggy and stopped crying.

"Ma-ma," the child cooed, extending his chubby arms to Maggy, who blanched self-consciously at the sight of the near-naked child suddenly claiming her as his mother.

"Not mama, Bobby," Cody corrected gently, corralling the child's chubby arms as he continued to reach for the stunned Maggy. "Come here, tiger," Cody growled, scooping the child out of Elizabeth's arms. He swung the toddler up on one lean hip and planted a kiss atop his head.

"*Bobby?*" Maggy mimicked weakly, staring at the duo in confusion. She took a step closer to Cody and the child as if she couldn't quite believe her eyes. "This…this is Bobby? The naked stranger with no teeth?" Her voice became a high-pitched croak as she turned to her mother.

"Why of course, dear," Elizabeth replied serenely.

Maggy sank down heavily on the couch as fiery waves of embarrassment washed over her. Oh Lord! Her mother had done it again! She'd lived with her mother and her peculiarities long enough to know that things weren't always what they seemed.

And *him*, she thought, glaring at Cody, who had the nerve to smile at her distress. He knew all along what she had been thinking. Why on earth hadn't he said something? Why had he let her go on making a fool of herself? One look at him and she had her answer. Obviously the man was having a good time at her expense. Her resentment grew.

On the other hand, she reasoned, it wasn't *his* fault she had jumped to conclusions. She was the one who had made a snap judgment, the one who had made such a blatant, obvious fool of herself. No wonder he found everything so amusing! If pressed, Maggy would have to admit her behavior was pretty funny. Not that she'd ever admit such a thing to him, though.

Smoothing down her skirt with shaking fingers, Maggy knew she had to swallow both her resentment and her pride and apologize to the man. What on earth must he think of her?

"Mr.—Cody," Maggy said, licking her lips nervously. "I think I owe you an apology." She tried hard to drag up a smile to match his.

"Apology accepted." Cody's deep voice vibrated with suppressed laughter, and Maggy flushed again.

"Oh Mother," she groaned. "I thought—well, I just assumed—why didn't you tell me Bobby was a child!" she demanded.

"Well, dear, you didn't ask." Elizabeth blew a tangle of silver curls out of her eyes as she plopped down on the couch.

"I thought…well…" Maggy struggled for words, fidgeting with her scarf. "I just assumed Bobby was a grown man with no teeth, no job, whose only interest was in the bottle and your money," she finished lamely, dropping her gaze to stare glumly at her shoes.

"A man!" Elizabeth's eyes twinkled. "Well, for goodness sake, dear! Whatever gave you that idea?" her mother asked innocently, trying hard not to smile. "I told you you've been working too hard."

"I'm sorry if I offended you," Maggy went on, feeling totally mortified. She watched Cody and the child in fascination. For some reason she found herself drawn to the man—and the child. Realizing she was staring, Maggy reluctantly dragged her eyes away. "All right, Mother. What's going on? I mean what's really going on?"

"I already told you, but apparently you weren't listening. Cody is an old and dear friend of mine, and right now he needs some help."

"What kind of help?" Maggy asked in sudden alarm, glancing from one to the other, and knowing she was probably going to be sorry she even asked. Her instincts immediately went on full alert. Long ago she had gotten used to her mother's penchant for high drama and adventure. Although she had been retired from the stage for years, she still had a flair for the dramatic. Not to mention the eccentric, Maggy thought, as the corners of her mouth twitched with humor. Her mother was totally guileless, outspoken and the only sixty-year-old radical she'd ever encountered.

Maggy knew that as long as there was a cause to support, a freedom to defend or an underdog in need of a champion her mother was happy. Glancing back at Cody, Maggy couldn't quite decide which of the three he was.

"Cody's in need of a—" All of a sudden Elizabeth grew tight-lipped. "Perhaps Cody'd better explain, dear."

Maggy's suspicions grew as the silence in the room lengthened. Why did she get the feeling her mother was about to drag her into another one of her adventures—or misadventures? Perhaps because it wouldn't be the first time. Her mother seemed to attract trouble the way dogs attracted fleas.

Taking a deep breath, Maggy tried to prepare herself for what was to come. Whatever her mother was involved in right now, it certainly couldn't be as bad as the time she had chained herself to a local theater scheduled for demolition, nor when she'd arranged a sit-in protest of the firing of a local cable television producer. Maggy stole another glance at Cody and the baby he was trying to entertain. On the other hand, maybe she'd better reserve judgment until she'd heard the man out.

"It's a long story," Cody finally said, releasing the child so that he could toddle over to Elizabeth. Maggy felt her nerves tighten. Experience had taught her that the longer the story, the worse it usually was. But after the way she had treated Cody, the only courteous thing to do was hear what he had to say.

Maggy reluctantly met Cody's gaze and was

caught short by his wolfish smile. She suddenly found herself breathless. He was looking at her— no, inspecting her—with such intense male interest that she nervously knotted her fingers together in her lap.

"I'm desperate, Maggy," he said sweetly, giving her a grin that should have sent her stampeding for the door. "Because right now, what I need is a *woman*!"

Chapter Two

Maggy's eyes flew to his. "Ex-excuse me?"

"A *woman*," Cody repeated, patiently specifying his need and trying earnestly—without much success—to banish the grin from the corners of his mouth.

For a long, silent moment, Maggy stared at him doubtfully, then her breath rose and fell in a great rush of relief. He was putting her on, she decided, having fun with her again, but this time it wasn't going to work. She was on to him. But she did have to hand it to the man. He was wild and outrageous and, Maggy admitted with a tinge of disgust, thoroughly charming in a brazen sort of way. But that didn't mean she was going to play straight man for him anymore. She could dish it out as well as take it.

"A woman," she deadpanned, straightening her spine against the couch and trying very hard to be blasé. "I see. Any particular kind of woman?" She was going to give back as good as she got, at least until she found out what the man *really* wanted.

"The usual kind—two legs, two arms, two—" he grinned again and her heart took an unexpected tumble "—well, you know."

Oh, she knew all right, but for the life of her she couldn't figure out why on earth he was telling *her*. Surely this man was quite capable of getting any woman he wanted, so why on earth was he informing her? Unless... A sudden thought occurred to Maggy, causing her nerves to begin an ominous squeal. He couldn't possibly mean—surely he didn't want a woman for—Maggy swallowed hard. Even he couldn't be that gauche? Could he?

"Would it be too much to ask what you *need* this woman for?" she asked carefully, praying her trembling voice didn't give away her thoughts.

"Well, it's not for what *you*'re thinking," Cody teased, and Maggy's heart settled back down in her chest, despite the fact that his tone was laced with devilish amusement. "I told you it was a long story. I'm a writer, you see, and—have you ever heard of a magazine called *Modern Motherhood*?"

Maggy shook her head. "I'm afraid I haven't."

"Well, about a year ago I started writing a series of articles for *Modern Motherhood*. You know, tips and advice for new mothers?" He was looking at her expectantly, and Maggy finally nodded her head as if she fully understood—which she didn't—and as if there were nothing out of the ordinary about this conversation or this man—which there was.

"Anyway," Cody continued. "Every year *Modern Motherhood* nominates one of their authors as Mother of the Year."

"So now you see the problem, dear." Elizabeth looked at Maggy, who in turn stared at her mother blankly.

"No, Mother, I'm afraid I don't." If there was a point to this conversation, she had obviously missed it.

"Maggy, do pay attention." Elizabeth tugged at the ribbon around her head as she struggled to contain Bobby. "Cody has been nominated as *Modern Motherhood*'s Mother of the Year."

"Congratulations," Maggy returned politely. Mother of the Year. Sure. Next they'd be telling her he could pull stars from the sky! And that the moon was made of yogurt. At this point nothing would surprise her. Maggy swallowed around her sudden nervousness. On second thought, maybe she'd better reserve judgment.

"There's an awards ceremony in Chicago next

month that Cody has to attend," Elizabeth explained patiently.

"And?" Maggy prompted, vividly aware that even her mother didn't see anything unusual about this conversation. Or this man. But then again, Maggy mused, her mother never did.

"That's what I need a woman for," Cody explained hurriedly at the dazed look on her face. "I need someone, a woman, to go to Chicago and accept that mothering award on my behalf."

"I offered to do it," Elizabeth sniffed, struggling to hang on to Bobby and talk at the same time. "But I don't think anyone would believe *I*'m the mother of a two-year-old. I look good for my age—" Elizabeth patted her hair "—but not that good."

"Why on earth would you need a woman for this?" Maggy asked, looking in confusion from one to the other. "Why can't you simply accept the award yourself?"

"Because," Cody said evasively, as if the word covered all the bases.

Maggy looked at him suspiciously. She had the feeling she was going to be sorry she even asked, but her curiosity got the best of her.

"Why not?"

He brought his gaze back to hers and Maggy's pulse jumped like a needle on a warped record. Those devilish blue eyes of his held a host of promises: adventure, humor, *recklessness*. She lowered her eyes, disconcerted now because every time she looked up, his eyes seemed to be waiting.

"Have you ever heard of Adventure Publications?" he finally asked.

"Here we go again," Maggy muttered. "Am I going to need a road map to follow this conversation?" she inquired with a raised brow.

"No, no, no," he said with a laugh, quickly trying to reassure her. "Listen, Mags, it's like this. I've authored a series of action and adventure books for Adventure Publications. *Wild Bill Cody's Adventures*," he announced proudly, and Maggy couldn't help but smile. She didn't know if she was smiling at the utterly ridiculous abbreviation of her name, or his animated tall tale.

"For years now I've cultivated a rough-and-tough macho image. It's what my stories demanded." Cody leaned forward in his chair, planted his feet flat on the floor and looked directly at her. "Now Mags, how would it look if my fans found out that *Wild Bill Cody*'s won a Mother of the Year Award?" His voice rose to a properly scandalized level, and Maggy's sense of humor overrode her exasperation.

"I simply can't imagine." She laughed.

"So you can *see* why I can't accept that award myself."

"Why, of course," Maggy returned solicitously, not seeing anything of the sort. Where on earth had her mother found this one? she wondered. She racked her brain for a way to get this handsome but rather peculiar man out of her mother's house. She didn't think he was dangerous, but clearly the man's bulb was short a few watts.

"See, my bosses at Adventure Publications aren't too thrilled that one of their leading writers has won a mothering award. Their message was pretty clear. If I accept that award myself my credibility as well as my career will be shot to—Haiti."

"So don't accept the award," Maggy countered, hoping he was at the end of this story, and deciding to humor him just in case he wasn't.

"I have to," Cody explained with maddening patience. "Part of the prize is a scholarship to college for Bobby." His face softened as his eyes found the child, and he smiled gently. "Hell, it would be reckless and irresponsible to just toss away something like that. This award could insure Bobby's future. And I'm sure I don't need to tell you how important a college education is?"

Maggy's gaze followed Cody's, and she looked at the child. It was clear that the bond between them was strong. Despite her misgivings about the man and his story, she had to admit there was something heartbreakingly old-fashioned about a big, rugged, supposedly macho man who was so obviously devoted to his child. She felt something tug at her heart.

Glancing up at Cody, she found herself smiling. She'd been hanging around her mother too long, she mused, because this whole ridiculous story was beginning to make sense to her.

If this man was telling the truth, and she'd reserve judgment for the moment, Maggy could see he really did have a problem. But on the other hand, it was *his* problem, and she had no idea why on earth he was telling her.

"I still don't see what all this has to do with me." She caught the glance Cody and her mother exchanged and dawning horror began to seep into her consciousness, growing stronger when Cody turned to her with a playful grin.

"Oh no!" Maggy breathed, shaking her head firmly. "Don't tell me you expect *me* to accept this mothering award for you?"

"Well, you don't have to act like I asked you to dance naked down Main Street," Cody pointed out, quite clearly offended at her tone of voice.

"Absolutely not," Maggy said firmly, shaking her head. He might just as well have asked her to dance naked down Main Street, because there was about as much chance of her doing one as the other. "There is no way," Maggy stammered, realizing immediately that this story was just crazy enough to be true. While she would willingly do anything for her mother, and had in the past, this was going too far, even for her. "It's not possible," she insisted.

"Why not?" Cody asked with a frown, obviously not paying any more attention to her protests than her mother ever did.

Why not? Indeed. How on earth did she ever expect a man like him to understand?

As the assistant headmistress at Miss Avalon's Academy for Young Ladies, Maggy's position decreed that she conduct herself in a manner befitting her vocation. Miss Avalon's was the most established, prestigious finishing school in the Midwest. Nestled in the rolling Wisconsin countryside, generation after generation of proper young ladies had been trained and educated at the academy, including Maggy herself. Her boss Miss Barklay, the headmistress of Miss Avalon's, demanded that her faculty be of the highest character and reputation. Maggy's actions both personally and professionally must be totally above reproach at all times. But how, she wondered, could she expect this man to understand when her own mother didn't?

Maggy knew she would have to approach this situation with great calm and deal with it in a logical manner—the way she dealt with everything else. Otherwise her mother and this man would have her entangled in another screwball scheme and Maggy couldn't afford it, not now. She tried to maintain a detached air, but it was hard with her mother staring, the toddler squirming, and a handsome blue-eyed rogue doing his best to drown her in his charm.

"I happen to be at a very sensitive stage of my career right now. I can't afford to become embroiled in—'' Maggy searched her mind for the correct phrase, then quickly rejected her choice for a more polite one ''—anything that might reflect badly on me or my position. I simply can't do it," she insisted, and both Cody and her mother stared at her. Neither said a word, but just kept looking at her until Maggy grew decidedly uncomfortable. "Well, I can't," she repeated, wondering why her voice suddenly sounded so feeble.

She could just see Miss Barklay's face if she learned that Maggy, her hand-picked successor, had suddenly announced to all the world that she was not only an author, but the unmarried mother of a two-year-old as well! Sweet heaven! Neither Miss Barklay nor the academy would ever recover. Nor would Maggy's career. No, there had to be another way.

"Surely you must know some woman who would be willing to accept this award for you?" Maggy asked.

Cody rubbed the back of his neck and flashed her a sheepish smile. "Well, Mags, to tell you the truth, the women I'm...uh...acquainted with aren't exactly motherly types." He wiggled his brows suggestively at the stunned look on her face. "If you know what I mean?"

Maggy felt a nervous twitch inch along her

mouth. Oh Lord, she knew all right! Why on earth was she so surprised? Cody certainly didn't look like the type of man to surround himself with modest women who cloaked and covered themselves from stem to stern, wore sensible shoes and practical undergarments.

Maggy glanced down and realized mournfully that she had just described herself. A flicker of defiance kicked up her spine. Why should she care if she wasn't his type? He wasn't her type either—not that she had a type—he was just too…too…male. Cody reminded her of the men of long ago, men who had braved the frontier to tame the Wild West. But the West wasn't wild anymore, and Maggy had a sinking feeling there wasn't anything tame about this man or his type of woman.

"Surely you could find someone on your own?" she muttered feebly.

Cody chuckled softly. "I already tried that, Mags. All I got for my trouble was a slap in the face, a kick in the shin and a bop on the head from a rampaging umbrella. Most women never let me finish explaining. As soon as I said I needed a woman and was willing to pay—well—all hell broke loose."

Maggy nodded her head. She could just imagine Cody sidling up to some poor innocent woman and then dropping his little proposition. He was lucky he hadn't gotten himself arrested!

"So you can see why Cody needs your help,

dear,'' her mother stated calmly. Maggy realized she had to put a stop to this. Immediately. She had lived with a deep-seated dread that one day her mother would get involved in something, or get *her* involved in something that could quite possibly ruin her career at Miss Avalon's. Cody and his harebrained scheme just might be the thing to do it.

''Mother,'' she said gently, genuine regret in her voice. ''I sympathize with Cody and his problem. But there's no way I can accept this award for him. Nor can I help him find a woman to do it. I wouldn't even know where to begin. Besides, it's just not logical, rational, or even sensible.'' She tried to soften her words. ''What he wants to do is very noble, and I sympathize with him, but I simply can't help.'' She saw the disappointment on her mother's face, and regret raced through her. If the blasted man's reasons hadn't been so darn honorable, she probably would have already tossed him out on his ear. But knowing *why* Cody wanted her help made it more difficult to say no.

Her mother clucked her tongue, and Bobby, who had been quietly playing on the floor, mimicked the sound, ''Dear.'' Her mother heaved a maudlin sigh. ''Must you be so logical and sensible all the time? It's a bit annoying, you know. If you're not careful, you'll become as persnickety as Miss Barklay.''

''Persnickety!'' Maggy's temper flared. They were not going to make her the proverbial bad guy in this little drama. Not this time. "Mother, you know very well if Miss Barklay—"

"Miss Barklay!" One silver brow rose as Elizabeth shuddered, drawing out the woman's name as if Henrietta Barklay were something that had crawled out of a long-closed jar. "That woman has the disposition of a goat! Come to think of it, she looks like one, too! I don't know why you let that woman intimidate you. What does she know about life? Nothing, absolutely nothing! Henrietta Barklay's been tiptoeing through life, hoping to get safely to her grave. And the way things are going she just might make it!" Sniffing loudly, Elizabeth let loose another mournful sigh, and Maggy had to resist the urge to roll her eyes toward the heavens. Her mother's theatrics were legendary, on and off the stage.

"Seems to me, dear, you'd listen to your own mother before you'd listen to her. Just for once, Maggy," her mother pleaded, her tone softening. "Can't you let your heart rule your head?"

It was an age-old battle that she and her mother'd had for years. While her mother lustily grabbed what life had to offer and ran with it, always letting her heart rule her head, Maggy tended to play it safe, letting her head rule her heart.

Because of the safety and security of her position at the academy, Maggy had never allowed herself to venture outside the structured boundaries of acceptable, correct behavior. She had been content, until now.

But watching her mother happily playing with Bobby, Maggy realized that just this once she'd like to be more like her mother. Just this once she'd like to do something without worrying about the consequences.

While she loved her job and her career, at times she resented the restrictions placed on her life, not just professionally but personally, as well. And this was one of those times, she realized, refusing to admit that her feelings had anything to do with the man sitting across the room from her with the mischievous smile and the devilish eyes.

She had always played by the rules, and it was clear that Cody, like her mother, was in the habit of breaking them.

Just this once...temptation taunted Maggy.

Then reason took over. She was tired of her mother treating her like the proverbial killjoy. Maggy glanced at her mother and felt her resolve tumble like pins in a bowling alley. Damn!

"I'm sorry, Mother," Maggy said quickly, before she could change her mind. Someone in this family had to keep their wits about them and remain calm and sensible, and quite clearly it wasn't going to be her mother. "I simply can't do it."

"Just this once, dear," her mother implored. "Couldn't you forget that hatchet-faced boss of—"

"Easy, Elizabeth, don't be so hard on her," Cody admonished, causing Maggy to look up at him in surprise. His blue eyes were waiting for hers, glistening in understanding. Maggy uttered a short sigh. The last thing she expected was for him to take her side. She couldn't help the sudden piquing of interest that welled up inside her or the rush of guilt. Why did doing the right thing suddenly make her feel so wrong?

"Maggy's got her reasons," Cody went on. "She's logical and sensible, and those are very admirable qualities." He flashed Maggy a conspiratorial wink as he pulled himself out of the chair. His movements were slow and deceptively casual, yet Maggy found she couldn't tear her eyes from Cody's rugged grace. His jeans clung in all the right places, and Maggy's heart did a free-fall as she watched him draw himself upright and stretch his long legs.

"I'm thirty-five years old," Cody went on, unaware of her scrutiny. "And I haven't done a logical, sensible thing in my life. I guess if I had I wouldn't have gotten myself into this mess in the first place. Now would I?"

Did he have to be so nice? Maggy wondered in disgust. She didn't want or need his understanding. If the man had gotten mad or furious, maybe then she wouldn't have felt so bad. As it was, she felt awful. She had let down her mother, probably robbed an innocent child of an education and disappointed a perfectly normal, charming man. And all in the space of one afternoon! Guilt washed over her like a morning shower.

"Mags," Cody said gently, crossing the room to stand in front of her. "Don't feel guilty."

Her eyes flew to his. How did he do that? she wondered crossly. He had read her thoughts as if they had sprouted legs and were marching single file across her forehead. "I understand. And so does your mother. Don't you, Elizabeth?" he prompted. Her mother gave a disdainful snort.

"Don't worry." Cody lifted her chin with one finger and Maggy's eyes reluctantly found his again. Shivers of delight rolled up her spine, leaving her feeling weak and warm. Taking a deep breath to clear her clouded brain, all she succeeded in doing was filling herself with his scent. No flowery perfume for this man. Cody smelled clean, fresh and totally male. "Bobby and I will manage," he promised, making Maggy swallow hard. "We always have." He smiled down at her. "I promised your mother here a night on the town, so if you don't mind, I guess I'll go get changed." With a wink, Cody pivoted on his heel and sauntered out of the living room. His loose-limbed stride caused his hips to roll in a way that was utterly appealing. Unable to drag her eyes away, Maggy watched him, allowing herself that one small pleasure. Oh, how this man could complicate her life, if she allowed it—which of course she wouldn't, she resolved firmly.

"Are you going to help Cody find a woman or not?" Elizabeth demanded after Cody had left.

"Mother." Maggy gingerly rubbed her now throbbing forehead. Her nerves felt as taut as the twine on a trussed turkey. "Please try to understand. I just can't."

"Are you sure?" Elizabeth inquired testily, rising with Bobby in her arms.

"Yes, Mother." Sighing, Maggy shook her head, trying to drive Cody's presence from her mind and to pay attention to her mother. "I'm sorry."

"Very well, dear. In that case I suggest you cancel your plans for tonight."

Maggy instantly came to attention, wondering what misadventure her mother had planned for her now.

"Why?" she queried, trying not to be suspicious.

"Because if *you're* not going to help Cody find a woman, *I am*. And the least you can do," Elizabeth said crossly, plopping Bobby in Maggy's lap, "is baby-sit!"

Chapter Three

"Baby-sit!" Maggy cried, struggling to get out of the chair and hold on to the child at the same time. "Mother! I'm not a nanny. And you know very well I don't know anything about—" Maggy frantically glanced down at Bobby "—babies," she finally whispered. She knew a lot about children, *school-children*, but literally nothing about the care of a toddler.

"Then maybe it's about time you learned," Elizabeth said sweetly, patting her daughter's cheek. "It will make you a well-rounded person, dear."

"I don't want to be a well-rounded—"

"Ma-ma," Bobby gurgled again, and Maggy stopped abruptly to look at the child. He really was beautiful, and she felt a tug at her heart, wondering where the child's real mother was. Bobby wound an arm around her neck, stuck his thumb in his mouth and snuggled close to her. Instinctively her arms enfolded him.

"What is he doing?" Maggy asked, fascinated.

"I believe he's sucking his thumb," Elizabeth replied smartly.

"Why doesn't he have any clothing on?" Maggy asked, her curiosity getting the best of her as she studied the near-naked child. He was so soft and warm and pink!

"Because he doesn't like clothing," Elizabeth informed her. "Now don't worry, dear, you're a reasonably intelligent, logical woman, surely even *you* can manage to take care of a baby for a few hours. Have a good evening, dear." Elizabeth turned and swept from the room, and Maggy developed an instant distaste for the word "logical."

"Mother!" she cried, holding Bobby as if he were a piece of fine china. "Mother! You can't be serious!" She knew her mother, and her instincts told her she was up to no good. Maggy didn't know which appalled her more: the fact that her mother and Cody were going to go gallivanting around town on their own, to do Lord knows what, or the fact that she was going to be left home, holding the... baby.

"Mother," Maggy called through clenched teeth. "This isn't funny. Mother!" She must have startled the child, because he let loose an ear-piercing wail. "Shh," she cooed, giving him an awkward pat on the bare backside. "Don't cry," Maggy implored. As his wails increased, he drove his fingers deep into the back of her hair, tangling the silky mane. "Please don't cry!" Maggy winced, trying to untangle his hands and soothe him at the same time. She realized almost immediately that patting his behind had been a mistake.

"Oh, my word!" Abruptly Maggy pulled her now damp hand away from Bobby's backside and gently eased him away from her. A dark, wet stain was racing across the front of her previously immaculate blouse and jacket. "Damn!" she whispered, wondering what he had done. Logically, she knew full well what he had done. All over her.

"Damn," Bobby repeated and Maggy's eyes widened. Good gracious, no one had ever told her babies were mimics! She had been with him all of two minutes and already had taught him a new word. This was not exactly a smashing beginning. A soggy beginning, perhaps, she mused as her sense of humor took over.

"Shh," she cautioned again, raising a finger to her lips. "You mustn't say that," she instructed, wondering what his father would say when he heard she had taught him a new word.

"Damn," Bobby repeated again with absolute delight.

Struggling not to laugh, Maggy marched into the kitchen for some paper towels. She peeled the child's reluctant arms away from her neck in order to sit him down on a chair. But once he was seated, Maggy realized that with his mobility it would only take a second for him to scramble down or fall. She couldn't take a chance on him getting hurt. Gingerly lifting his bottom off the chair, she decided to seat him on the floor. "Sit here for a minute, would you, Sport?"

Bobby favored her with a smile, and she hesitantly smiled back. He really was a very cute kid, she decided. Wet, but cute.

Grabbing a wad of paper towels, Maggy shrugged out of her suit coat, kicked off her pumps and tried to dry off her blouse as best she could. Dissatisfied with the job, she loosened her scarf and sent it sailing in Bobby's direction. "Here, Sport, this ought to keep you busy while I clean myself up." Bobby tried to catch the scarf in midair, his chubby fingers catching just enough of it to send it sailing again. He crawled after it, giggling happily as he went.

Satisfied that the child would be occupied for at least the next few minutes, Maggy undid the first three buttons of her blouse. Keeping an eye on the child, she blotted the fabric inside and out, then reached down for Bobby to dry him off, too. Lifting him in the air, she wrinkled her nose as she got a good whiff of him. "No offense, Sport." She chuckled. "But you smell like a puppy. I think you need a bath."

"Baff," Bobby gurgled.

"Mother?" she called, to no avail. "Mother!" Realizing she had been left alone to sink or swim, Maggy looked around the kitchen. Her vast education hadn't included Babies 101 and she had no idea what to bathe him in. The bathtub was out of the question. The tub was too big and Bobby too small. She was willing to admit that the idea of placing the small child in a large tub filled with water scared her senseless. What if he slipped? What if he swallowed water? Certainly a child his size needed something a bit smaller.

"Baff, now!" Bobby demanded, trying to squirm loose from her arms.

"In a minute, Sport." Maggy crossed the kitchen, and holding Bobby like a football, she dropped the stopper in the sink and turned on the water, filling the sink halfway. It wasn't perfect, but it would have to do. Testing the water with a finger and satisfied that it was suitable, she gingerly placed the toddler in the sink.

Certainly even she could manage to give a child a bath, she reassured herself. After all, she'd been bathing herself for twenty-five years without any catastrophes. Bathing a baby certainly couldn't be any more difficult. Could it?

As Maggy grabbed a bar of soap, Bobby's chubby

fingers reached out for the uncapped bottle of dish detergent. He tightened his fingers around the plastic bottle and Maggy let out a squeal as a crooked stream of soap and bubbles assaulted her.

"Bobby!" she cried, trying to hang on to him and grab the bottle at the same time.

He giggled gleefully, twisting his hands out of her reach. He was having too much fun to let go of his new toy.

"Please release that!" Maggy cried, trying without success to release Bobby's grip. Her hands were wet and her grasp slippery. It wasn't until he had sprayed her hair, face and most of her blouse that she managed to wrestle the bottle away from him.

"More bubbles," he wailed, slapping and splashing her with water.

"No more bubbles," she said firmly, ducking the steady stream of water he sent in her direction. Blowing a wad of soggy blond hair out of her eyes, Maggy quickly soaped the child down and rinsed him off.

"Out we go, Sport," she announced, grabbing Bobby firmly under the arms and lifting him out of the sink.

"More baff," Bobby insisted, waving his wet arms and kicking his feet.

"No more baff—I mean bath," she corrected. "You're sufficiently clean," she announced imperiously, trying to use her arms to wipe at her eyes.

"And so am I." She gave his little body a gentle shake, and then realized that although he had smelled like a puppy, it would take a good deal more than a shake to get him dry. But what was she supposed to dry him with? she wondered, as she cradled his soaked body against her.

Her eyes darted frantically around the kitchen. A dish towel was hanging from a rack, but it was across the room. In order to retrieve it she'd have to hang on to Bobby, keep her balance on the floor that was now streaked with water and cross the room with the child in tow without falling. No, she decided, with a shake of her head, it was much too far and she was too inexperienced even to attempt such a fate.

Grabbing the roll of paper towels, Maggy ripped off several sheets. "This will have to do, Sport," she announced, handing him the roll of toweling to keep him occupied. Immediately she realized it was the wrong thing to do. With her hands full of him, Bobby proceeded to unroll the paper toweling.

"Stop!" Maggy cried, fighting her way out from under a mountain of paper and wondering how anyone with only two hands ever managed to give a baby a bath.

"Sport eat now?" Bobby asked, yawning and looking up at her with wide blue eyes.

"In a minute, honey," Maggy said, reaching out to brush his dark hair out of his eyes. She was surprised at how downy soft his hair was and threaded her fingers through it again. For a moment she looked at him as a strange feeling took flight inside her. She had heard and read all about maternal longings, particularly in women of her age, but until this moment had never imagined them affecting her. She had been so busy in her career that the idea of a family and a home of her own had never really meant anything to her. Until now.

Without thinking, she lifted Bobby close, burying her nose in the warm cavern of his neck just to see what it would feel like. He was so soft and smelled so sweet. Gently she kissed the folds of his neck, then kissed him again as he let loose a giggle.

"Sport eat now?" he repeated, pulling away. Maggy chuckled softly.

"Yes, Sport eat now."

"Damn," Bobby repeated, as she walked barefoot to the refrigerator. Maggy laughed again, hugging Bobby close.

Deciding it was best not to admonish him or repeat his new word, she opened the refrigerator door and searched for something suitable for him to eat. What *did* one feed a two-year-old? She didn't even know if he had any teeth. If her mother was to be believed, he didn't.

"I don't suppose you'd open your mouth so I could see what's inside, would you?" Maggy asked, laughing at her own outrageousness. She didn't really expect the child to answer her, but it certainly wouldn't hurt to ask.

"Nothing special in his mouth, Mags," Cody announced from the doorway. "Nothing, that is, except teeth. He's got quite a few, so I don't recommend you put your fingers anywhere near because he just might take a bite. He can be cranky when he's hungry." Cody grinned as his eyes slowly took inventory of her disheveled state. "He takes after me," he said slowly, and Maggy's heart stalled somewhere in her chest.

"I see." She was uneasy at being caught in such a condition. Self-consciously she looked down at herself. Her feet were bare, and while her skirt was relatively unharmed, her blouse was half open, revealing a great deal more of her feminine charms than she cared to have exposed—not that it mattered. Her white blouse was so wet that it clung provocatively to her slender frame, outlining every inch of her curves beneath her practical cotton lingerie.

"What happened in here?" Cody asked with a smile that sent her heart crashing against the walls of her chest. Cody was looking at her in a way that made her nerves pop like corn in a hot skillet. She dropped her gaze and quietly observed him. He had changed his clothes, and although he wasn't exactly wearing a three-piece suit, the dark gray slacks and crisp white shirt he wore looked more devastating than any business suit she'd ever seen.

"I...I gave Bobby a bath," she said, hastily trying to pull her clothing together as Cody crossed the room. "I hope you don't mind."

Laughing softly, Cody playfully chucked Bobby on the chin. Although he was talking to Bobby, his eyes were relentlessly searching hers. "Looks like *you*'re the one who got the bath. What on earth did you do to our Mags, here?" he asked the child, holding out his arms. The words *our Mags* reverberated through her mind, sending a shiver through her nervous system. What would it be like to belong to this man? Maggy wondered wistfully. And this child? A sense of longing enveloped her.

"Maybe you had better close that door before something spoils," Cody suggested with a grin, as he nodded toward the refrigerator door that Maggy was holding on to for dear life.

"Oh!" She slammed the door shut, feeling rattled again.

"I came in here to thank you," he said, lifting a finger to brush a wet strand of hair from her cheek. Without her shoes, she had to tilt her head to look at Cody, and he seemed even more imposing.

"To thank me?" she said absently, touching her skin where just a moment before his finger had been.

"Your mother told me you offered to baby-sit Bobby tonight."

Maggy didn't see any reason to point out to him that she hadn't exactly *offered* her services, that she'd been conned, or rather bullied. But now it was a matter of pride. The fact that her mother had hinted that she couldn't take care of a baby even for one evening had been just enough of a challenge for Maggy to prove that she could.

Maggy detested being told she wasn't capable of accomplishing something. It just made her more determined to prove them wrong. She'd faced challenges all her life. Someone always seemed to be telling her she couldn't do something, whether it was taking Latin in school, competing on the college track team or becoming headmistress. Maggy was now fluent in Latin, had been the star of her college track team, and she knew the position of headmistress was now within her grasp.

Inexperienced or not, Maggy was going to take care of Bobby tonight—if he didn't do her in first.

Cody's eyes pinned hers. "I want you to know how much I appreciate it."

"That's all right," she managed to say. "I appreciate you taking my mother out for the evening. She hasn't been out all that much since my father died—"

"I was sorry to hear about your father," Cody said softly, and something in his voice made her look up at him in surprise. "He was a good man."

"I know," she said, unable to drag her eyes from

his. Lord, she thought, he had the most glorious eyes. Gathering her senses, Maggy decided to get back to a more neutral subject. "Cody, I think I'd better warn you about Mother," she said with a sudden frown, and he chuckled softly.

"I know all about your mother. We go way back. I got to know your mother when I first started writing. I did a story on her right after she retired from the theater. She helped me launch my career." Cody smiled at the look on Maggy's face. Her mother had helped so many people over the years, in more ways than she could count. Maggy respected her mother enormously, despite her penchant for the dramatic.

"Hey!" Cody tapped her on the chin, and she blinked up at him. "What were you going to tell me about your mom? Some kind of warning, I believe?" There was just a hint of mischief in his eyes and Maggy began to wonder if Cody and her mother were birds of a feather. Good Lord, she had a hard enough time keeping her mother out of trouble without worrying about him, too.

"Mother is a bit…outrageous at times. She tends to do and say things that occasionally get her in hot water. As long as you're escorting her this evening, I thought perhaps you might keep an eye on her, just to make sure she stays out of trouble."

"Come on, Mags. A little trouble never hurt anybody," he teased. "Makes life worth living."

"Still," she said worriedly, "I'd appreciate it if

you'd keep an eye on her. She's not as young as she thinks she is. Oh, and another thing,'' Maggy added, ''under no circumstances are you to let her talk you into going to the Boom Boom Club.''

''The Boom Boom Club?'' Cody repeated, his voice clearly indicating more interest than she would've liked. One dark brow shot up, and he grinned. ''What's that?''

''It's kind of a...bar,'' Maggy hedged, wondering how she was going to explain what the club was without dying of embarrassment in the process. The Boom Boom Club was on the outskirts of town, and featured amateur strip nights as well as topless waitresses and waiters, not to mention other such nonsense. Her mother had been dying to get a look at the place for months, much to Maggy's distress.

''They serve food,'' she continued, despite the look on his face. ''And it...has entertainment.''

''Doesn't sound so bad to me, Maggy,'' he said, his eyes gleaming wickedly. ''What kind of entertainment are we talking about?''

''Just...entertainment,'' she said hesitantly, too embarrassed to go into specifics, and realizing Cody knew *exactly* what kind of place they were talking about.

''Ahh,'' he drawled slowly, nodding his head while trying to extract Bobby's fingers from his pocket. ''Sounds like a strip joint to me.'' He grinned. "Don't be embarrassed, Mags. We've got a few of them back home in Tennessee, too."

And no doubt he had made a personal inspection of each and every one. Maggy decided to change the subject. "Cody, I hope you understand why I can't help you with your problem." She looked into his eyes, searching for some hint of understanding.

"You've got your reasons. But you must understand, I've got mine, too. Bobby's education is very important to me."

Maggy nodded. "I understand," she said softly. And oddly enough Maggy did understand. *She* just couldn't help him. But a thought suddenly occurred to her. "Cody, what about your wife?"

"My what?" He looked at her wildly and it was Maggy's turn to smile.

"Your wife," she repeated, and Cody threw back his head and let loose a great peal of laughter, startling Bobby who started to cry and reach for Maggy. She took the child, cradling him close and whispering soothing words, all the while wondering what on earth Cody found so funny.

"Forgive me for laughing, Maggy," he finally managed, wiping at his eyes. The twinkle remained. "But I guess you could say I'm an...unwed father."

"What?" she asked blankly, trying to stop the thoughts that were storming through her brain. Cody was a Mother of the Year, an unwed father, and the women he knew weren't motherly types. So where on earth did Bobby come from? At this point she was unwilling to rule out the stork. After all these years of living with her mother, it was certainly a reasonable possibility. Knowing her mother and her friends, *anything* was a possibility.

"No, it's not at all what you're thinking," he said again, startling her with his perceptiveness. "I haven't got a wife. In fact I've never been married. Bobby's my sister Pearl's boy." Cody rushed on. "She ran off with a game-show host and left Bobby with me."

"Bobby's not your son?" she asked.

"Nephew," Cody explained, looking at the child with a soft expression.

"Did she really run off with a game-show host?" Maggy whispered despite herself, and Cody chuckled.

"Well, he wasn't really a game-show host. But he sure looked like one. You know the type— smooth, real smooth. The guy had shiny suits, slicked-back hair and a big toothy grin that seemed pasted on his lips. Pearl ran off and left Bobby with me when he was barely a year old. I'm his legal guardian now."

"I'm sorry," Maggy stammered, not knowing what else to say. "I had no idea. I just assumed." She couldn't believe this man would take on the responsibility of raising a child that wasn't even his own, protecting him from life's harsh reality, per-

haps at his own expense. Cody was a very special
man, a man of rare integrity and honesty. It was very
refreshing.

"It's all right. I don't go around advertising that
he's not my boy. It doesn't make a whit of difference to me, or to him. I've had him ever since he
learned to talk, and it just seemed easier for him to
call me Daddy. Uncle Cody's kind of hard for his
little mouth to master." Cody scratched the back of
his neck. "The only problem is, he's at an age now
where he calls every woman he sees mama. But
we'll work it out, he and I. We'll do just fine, don't
you worry." He looked down at her earnestly, and
Maggy met his gaze. For the first time in a very
long while, a man was treating her like a woman
and not like a respected, distinguished member of
Miss Avalon's Academy. She could see it in his
eyes, feel it in the air between them. It made her
feel small, feminine and special—not to mention in-
credibly guilty.

"What are you going to do?" she asked, wondering if she had been too abrupt in her refusal to
help him.

Cody looked at her long and hard. "Well, I'm not
going to worry about it, that's for sure. Right now
I'm going to have some dinner with your mother,
maybe talk about old times. Then tomorrow, Bobby
and I, we'll be on our way." He shrugged offhand-
edly, but his gaze was on her. She felt the intensity

of his eyes, questioning, probing, and she suddenly knew how a butterfly felt, trapped behind a glass case.

Tomorrow he would be gone, she thought. Almost as if he'd never been. But he had been. And she knew she'd remember him for a long, long time. There was something honest, open, and heart-touchingly old-fashioned about the man. And something very, very appealing, her mind echoed.

"Mags, don't you worry on my account, please?" He lifted her chin with his fist, and she dared to look at him. Startled by what she saw there, she dropped her gaze to the hollow of his throat. A patch of thick, curly hair peeked out from beneath the material, and she wondered for a moment what it would be like to run her fingers through it. Would it be as soft as little Bobby's? Probably, she decided.

"Maggy?" Cody's deep voice was a soft caress that made her knees grow weak again. For a moment she was afraid to actually look at him, but then, with a sigh, she met his gaze. "Are you sure you can manage here tonight? With Bobby and all? It wouldn't be any trouble to take him with us."

"I can manage," she whispered, not certain at the moment just what she was agreeing to manage. There was an electricity about Cody that seemed to draw her. She wasn't skilled in this type of man/woman thing.

"Sport eat now?" Bobby looked up at her hopefully, instantly breaking the tension between her and Cody. They both laughed self-consciously, looking in relief at the child.

"Sport eat now," Cody confirmed, leaning forward to ruffle his hair.

"Speaking of Sport, what *does* he eat?" Maggy asked.

"Mostly soft finger foods, things he can eat with his hands without too much effort. And no matter how charming he is, don't give him any peanut butter. It sticks to the roof of his mouth and makes him cluck like a hen with dentures. And no grapes," he added. "He tends to choke on the seeds."

"Apes?" Bobby asked, beaming up at Maggy with a hopeful smile.

"No apes," Cody insisted, his voice gentle but firm.

"Damn." Bobby's mouth immediately turned downward, and Maggy's face flamed.

Cody looked at the child in surprise. "Boy, where'd you learn that word?" Cody asked sternly. "I'm sorry, Mags, I didn't teach him to talk like that."

"I'm sorry, Cody," Maggy stammered. "I—I— he heard me say it."

Cody tried not to smile. He couldn't imagine this woman using such language. "I think he's about done in for the day, Mags. I don't think he'll give you too much trouble."

She glanced down. "I'm sure we'll be fine. Oh, what about clothes? I don't think it's a good idea for him to waltz around naked."

A flush crept slowly up Cody's rough features and he grinned sheepishly. "That's my fault. He takes after me. I hate clothes, too. I rarely wear any, unless of course I'm in public. I guess he just picked up the habit. But I'll leave some pajamas in the living room for you."

She nodded, not trusting herself to make a comment on the subject. The image of Cody naked was one she didn't really feel ready to deal with, although the vision wafted through her mind.

"Well, I guess if you've got everything covered, I'll be going. I'll call you. Just to check in on him," he added, and her spirits plummeted. She'd thought he was going to be calling *her*.

He leaned closer to her, and for a moment her heart beat a wild cadence. She caught just a whiff of his male scent. A very pleasant scent, she decided, as Cody brushed his lips gently across the baby's forehead.

His eyes fastened on hers. "Good night, now."

"Good night," Maggy whispered, watching as Cody turned on his heel and walked out the door.

"Da night?" Bobby asked and she nodded, opening the refrigerator door again. She had to stop thinking about Cody and concentrate on Bobby. Right now, the only thing that should be occupying her mind was what to feed this child. But it wasn't. The only thing on her mind was a big, broad, gentle mountain of a man named Wild Bill Cody.

Chapter Four

"Bobby honey, the food is supposed to go in your mouth, not on the floor." Maggy laughed, trying to grab a piece of chicken as it went sailing from his hands. There was more food on the floor than in the child's stomach. Determined not to take any chances, Maggy had cut the cold chicken into tiny pieces. Even Bobby couldn't choke on them. In fact, he had trouble hanging on to them.

After gathering some old telephone books, Maggy had assembled a makeshift high chair for the child. She had laced a belt securely around Bobby's waist, weaving one end through the rungs of the chair. As long as she was going to baby-sit Bobby tonight, she was going to make sure that nothing happened to him. She planned to stick to him like summer underwear.

"More?" she asked, holding up a spoonful of gelatin.

Bobby nodded his head and opened his mouth, only to spit the gelatin all over her once he had it in his mouth. "Done," he announced, yanking off his makeshift bib.

"I wish you would have told me that before." Laughing, she grabbed a napkin and picked bits of cherry gelatin off her blouse.

"Let's clean you up, Sport." After dampening a rag, Maggy wiped off Bobby's hands and his mouth, bending to plant a kiss on the top of his head.

"Sport night-night." Yawning, he lifted his arms to her. After unassembling his chair, Maggy scooped him up in her arms and carried him into the living room. Since her house wasn't equipped with a crib, Maggy had gathered several blankets and pillows, improvising a bed for the child on the couch.

"Tired, Sport?" she asked, settling herself on the couch. Humming softly, she gently rocked Bobby, growing drowsy herself as the soothing motion relaxed her. Within a few moments Bobby had fallen asleep.

Silently Maggy watched him, a satisfied smile on her face. He really was a sweet child. Very good-tempered, which surprised her. She had always heard that children his age tended to be unmanageable. But except for the scene at bath time he'd been a perfect angel.

Cody had already called twice to check on him, and had been happy to learn that Bobby was behaving.

Leaning her head back against the couch, Maggy closed her eyes and let her thoughts drift. What a peculiar day this had been, she thought drowsily. Never in a million years could she have guessed when she left school this afternoon that she would be baby-sitting a toddler this evening.

With a soft sigh, Maggy settled herself more comfortably on the couch, grabbing a corner of an afghan to cover herself as she tucked her legs beneath her. Taking care of a child was hard work. Fun, but nerve-racking at times. She wondered how Cody did it.

Cody. A smile touched her lips as his image floated through her mind. It had been a long, long time since she had been impressed by a man. Most of the men she ran across were faculty. Maggy had never realized how much she missed being appreciated for her femininity until today—until she met Cody.

The ringing of the phone startled her out of her thoughts and she gently laid Bobby down on the couch before making a lunge for the phone.

"Hello," she whispered, keeping one eye trained on the child.

"Why are you whispering? Is something wrong with Bobby?"

"Cody? Is that you?" There was so much noise in the background that she could hardly hear him.

"It's me, Maggy. How's Bobby?" he asked.

"He's fine. He's already asleep. Cody? Where are you? What's all that noise?" she asked suspiciously.

Cody was silent for a moment. "Well Mags, I'm glad things are going well with you. Your mother and I—well—we've run into a little problem."

"Problem?" Her nerves tightened. "Cody, is Mother all right? Did something happen to her?" Her breathing slowed as she paced the space in front of the telephone table.

"No, nothing happened to your mother. She's fine, in fact she's right here."

Her breath came out in a relieved rush. "Thank goodness. Can I speak to her then?"

The background noise increased. "I'm afraid that's going to be a bit of a problem, Maggy. At least at the moment."

"Why?" Maggy frowned. "Cody, what's going on?"

"Now don't get upset," he cautioned.

"I won't get upset," she assured him. "Just tell me what's happened."

"Well, remember that restaurant you and I talked about?"

"Restaurant?" she repeated blankly, casting a

quick glance at Bobby who was still sleeping. "What restau—?" Her eyes widened. "Don't tell me you mean the Boom Boom Club!"

"You remember," he said with just enough cheerfulness to make her mad.

"Do you mean to tell me you and my mother are at the Boom Boom Club!"

"No. Now you said you wouldn't get upset on me, Mags," he reminded her. "We're not at the Boom Boom Club."

"Good." Maggy blew out a sigh of relief.

"Anymore."

"Anymore!" she cried, her voice rising into the receiver. "Cody, where are you?"

"Jail."

"What!" Her pacing grew faster. "Oh my God, Cody—what on earth—how did—when—Cody!" she cried again, twisting the cord into tiny little curls.

"Well, honey," he was whispering now, obviously covering the mouthpiece with his hand, because she could hear every quick intake of his breath. "Your mother and I were just minding our own business watching the show—"

"You were *what*!"

"Watching the show," he repeated calmly, as if they had been previewing Paris's latest fashions, instead of the town's own version of the *Folies Bergères*, "and the next thing I knew reporters and the police were there along with a half dozen picketers. Anyway the police tried to stop the picketers, and well—your mother tried to stop the police, and I tried to stop your mother." He paused for a breath. "Anyway, that's the long and the short of it."

"Oh Lord," Maggy whimpered.

"Now you promised you weren't going to get upset," he reminded her gently.

"I'm not upset!" she yelled.

"Uh, Mags. We've got another little problem."

"You call getting arrested a *little* problem?" Maggy shouted. "Losing a button is a little problem, Cody. Getting arrested is—"

"Now honey, calm down," he soothed. "Here's the problem. Seems they won't take a check for our bail money. Your mom and I—we need a hundred in cash—each—to get out of here, and I'm...ah...a little short of cash right now."

"Cody," Maggy said with a frown. "My mother should have enough cash—"

"No she doesn't," he said abruptly, too abruptly for Maggy's peace of mind. She knew for a fact her mother never went out with less than several hundred dollars in her purse.

"What do you mean she doesn't?"

"Well, she did have some cash, but she doesn't anymore," he repeated vaguely.

"Cody," Maggy said slowly, trying to hold on to what was left of her patience—and her sanity.

"What do you mean she did have, but she doesn't?" This conversation was reminiscent of their initial one, Maggy noted, realizing Cody would get to the point in his own good time, despite the fact that she was ready to throw back her head and scream with impatience.

There was a long pause before Cody spoke again. "She kind of gave it to one of the...dancers."

"What do you mean she gave her money to one of the *dancers*?"

"Well." Cody paused again. "She tucked it into the waistband of his costume. Mags, you should have seen her! She was having such a good time. She was laughing—"

"She tucked money into a man's...*what*!"

"Waistband," he repeated quickly. "Now you said you wouldn't get upset."

"I'm not upset," she cried. "I'm furious!"

"Mags," he said, his voice low and soothing as if he were talking to two-year-old Bobby, and not to a fully grown woman. "Calm down. It's not as bad as it seems."

Oh Lord, it was worse!

"Does this mean you're not going to bail us out?"

Maggy could hear the humor in his voice. Oh, how tempting!

Banishing the thought, she sighed heavily. "All

right.'' She rubbed a throbbing spot above her brow. ''Cody, listen to me. You stay there. I'll—''

''I don't reckon we're going anywhere.'' He chuckled softly and Maggy scowled. She didn't see anything particularly funny about the situation. But now didn't seem the time to point that out to him. Right now she had to get her mother and him out of jail.

''I'll be right down. Cody, *please*,'' she implored, knowing she was wasting her breath because he probably wouldn't listen to her anyway. ''Don't talk to *anyone*. And don't let Mother talk to anyone, either.'' His soft laughter filled her ears.

''What do you suggest I do, gag her?'' Maggy seriously considered the idea. For a moment.

''No. Just tell her I said not to talk to anyone until I get there.''

''See you in a bit then.'' The phone went dead, and Maggy slammed down the receiver. Her own mother in jail! Lord, Miss Barklay would have a certified fit if she learned about this!

''Mother,'' she raged, shaking her fist impotently in the air. Realizing she didn't have time to stand there lamenting, Maggy raced through the house, rummaging through her purse to see how much cash she had available.

One hundred and eighty-four dollars. ''Damn!'' she muttered, biting her lip and wondering what she was going to do.

Rushing to her bedroom, Maggy headed for the corner where a heavy jar filled with coins sat. Her father had taught her early in life the value of saving for a rainy day. Ever since she was a child she had been saving coins. Pennies, primarily. She looked at the jar carefully. There had to be at least a hundred dollars in change—probably more. The jar was too heavy to lift and her eyes darted around as she tried to figure out what to put the money in. Yanking down a large straw bag from her closet, Maggy began scooping coins out of the jar and shoving them in the bag. Satisfied she had enough, she slung the bag over her shoulder, raced through the house, grabbed her car keys off the table and slammed out the front door.

A moment later she was back. Lord! She had forgotten about Bobby.

"Sport," she whispered, shaking him gently. "Sport?"

Bobby's eyes fluttered open, and he looked at her as if he'd never seen her before. "Da-da?"

"No, not dada," she whispered, kissing him gently before scooping him, blankets and all, into her arms. "It's Maggy, honey. But we're going to go get your dada."

"Da-da," he repeated sleepily as she tried to maneuver him, the bag and herself to the car. Once settled, she strapped Bobby securely in the front seat, where he promptly snuggled in and fell right back to sleep.

Sighing in mock despair, Maggy maneuvered her car through the now quiet city streets. Her mother, in jail! How on earth could Cody have allowed this to happen?

In the space of a few hours a big, burly, devilish rogue had invaded her quiet life, upset their peaceful existence, made ridiculous demands, and now had somehow managed to get her mother thrown in jail. When she got her hands on him—well, Maggy wasn't quite sure what she was going to do, but surely she would think of something!

She made the half-hour trip to the police station in record time, parking right in front of the building, despite the fact that it was a no-parking zone.

Blinking sleepily once or twice, Bobby offered no resistance as she lifted him from the car and carried him into the station along with the bag of pennies.

The station was in chaos. Obviously the raid had netted a lot more people than just her mother and Cody. Scantily clad men and women paraded around, laughing and talking. Picketers, still waving their signs, vied for the attention of the reporters who had gathered to duly report all the goings-on. Deliberately Maggy ducked her head and evaded a reporter with a camera. The last thing she wanted was her picture in the paper. Maggy stepped behind a rather rotund man in a wild print shirt, hoping that the reporters wouldn't pay any attention to her.

"Da-da," Bobby whimpered, and Maggy stroked his head gently, comforting him in low, soothing tones. Obviously he wasn't used to so many people and was growing more agitated by the moment.

The rotund man finally finished at the desk and moved aside. Maggy, juggling Bobby in one arm, lifted her purse and the straw bag to the counter in order to count out the money.

"Rob the kid's piggy bank?" the officer on duty asked with a smile. While she struggled to keep Bobby quiet and happy, the officer at the desk counted all the change. Finally, satisfied that the exact amount of the bail had been paid, he handed a slip of paper to another officer, who headed down the hall.

"Send out Magee and Cody," he shouted, and Maggy winced as she moved to one side to wait for her mother and Cody. If she'd wanted her mother's name broadcasted all over the police station she would have rented a bullhorn! Right now all she wanted was to get her mother and get out of here. Cody, on the other hand, was another matter. She had quite a few things to say when she got her hands on him!

Her pulse jumped as she caught sight of him. He was hard to miss, since he stood head and shoulders above everyone else. He was lumbering down the hall with her mother tucked securely under his arm. At least neither of them looked any worse for their experiences, Maggy thought in relief. Bobby spotted Cody and immediately began to wail. Cody's face lit up when he caught sight of her and Bobby.

"Da-da," Bobby blubbered, struggling to get free of Maggy.

"Hi, Mags." Cody flashed her a blinding smile and lifted the baby into his arms. Maggy glared at him. He was *not* going to charm his way out of this little fiasco!

"Don't you *hi* me," she hissed out of the corner of her mouth, resisting the urge to give him a good whack just for good measure. "Cody, how could you?"

"Now, you promised you wouldn't get upset." He leaned down and pressed his face close to hers. "You're not upset, are you?" He grinned into her furious features.

"I'm not upset!" she lied, clenching her teeth in an effort not to yell at him. She was more upset by his nearness than by anything else at the moment. "How could you do this?"

He reached up and scratched his eyebrow, grinning sheepishly. "It wasn't all that hard—"

"What's that supposed to mean?" Maggy cried, annoyed that he didn't appear to be the least bit concerned about the evening's events. "Do you realize that in the—"

"Dear." Elizabeth sighed dramatically and patted Maggy's arm. Maggy wasn't sure if her mother was trying to divert her attention or stop her tirade. "How nice of you to come down and get us! This really is an *awful* place," her mother announced with unnecessary loudness. "The accommodations here are absolutely dreadful. Why, you should see the colors of the walls! It's so depressing—"

Maggy let out a long sigh. "Mother, this is a jail, not a country club. I'm sure no one really cares that you find the color of the walls depressing."

"Well," her mother huffed. "Someone should care."

"Mother, please?"

"And there's no privacy," her mother went on, totally ignoring Maggy's exasperation. "We really must speak to the legislators, perhaps a march on Washington—"

"No!" Maggy said quickly. "We're not going to speak to anyone about anything!" She could just see her mother organizing a march on Washington! Hadn't she had enough excitement for one evening? Maggy had to nip this in the bud, or before she knew it she'd be seeing her mother in leg irons on the evening news! Maggy rubbed her aching head. "Could we discuss the penal accommodations some other time? I'd like to go home now."

"Why, of course dear." Elizabeth smiled. "I'm a bit tired, anyway."

Taking the arm Cody offered, Elizabeth swept out the door. Staring glumly at their retreating backs, Maggy turned on her heel and followed them out, muttering under her breath.

"Here, Mags." Cody tried to hide a smile as he slid something across the windshield toward her. Glaring at him, Maggy snatched the piece of paper out of his hand and groaned. On top of everything else, she now had a parking ticket! All these years of driving and she'd never been ticketed until now! Clenching her teeth, Maggy climbed behind the wheel and started the car.

She was silent on the way home, preferring to concentrate on her driving rather than dwell on what she was going to do to the dangerous duo when she got them home.

Cody and her mother chatted amiably, and Maggy deliberately kept her eyes fastened on the road. Occasionally she glanced in her rearview mirror, but every time she did, Cody's mischievous eyes seemed to be waiting for her. It was clear that neither her mother nor Cody saw anything unusual about their evening's activity. Maggy wasn't certain what bothered her more, the fact that they'd been arrested or the fact that neither of them seemed in the least bit concerned about it!

Once inside the house, Maggy dropped her keys and purse on the table, and waited until Cody had

Bobby safely tucked into his temporary crib on the couch before confronting them.

"All right, I want to talk to both of you," she said, trying to drag up some of her anger again. She looked from one to the other, and they exchanged furtive glances.

"What about, dear?" her mother inquired innocently, and Maggy struggled to hold on to her patience.

"May I ask just what the devil you two were doing at the Boom Boom Club?"

"Before or after the police came?" her mother asked, and Maggy gnashed her teeth.

"Now Mags," Cody said, dropping down on the sofa right next to her. Bobby was at the other end, which meant that Cody sat closer to her than she would have liked. He was so close that she could feel the warmth of muscular thigh pressed against her. It raised a rash of goose bumps along her skin. "Don't be mad. It wasn't your mother's fault. It was mine."

"Nonsense!" Elizabeth interjected, giving her daughter a haughty look. "If you want to blame someone, Maggy, you might start with yourself."

"Me!" She gasped. "Are you trying to tell me it was my fault the two of you got arrested?"

"Frankly dear, yes." Her mother looked at her intently. "If you had agreed to help Cody none of this would have happened. It really was your fault."

"My fault!" Maggy burst out, unwilling to let her mother pass the buck this time. "What on earth does Cody finding a woman have to do with you getting arrested?" She couldn't wait to hear this explanation!

Her mother let out a put-upon sigh. "Well, dear, if *you* had agreed to help Cody find a woman, then I wouldn't have had to."

"Mother," Maggy said slowly, her tone incredulous. "Are you trying to tell me that you went to a—a strip joint in order to find a woman for Cody!"

"Of course, dear. Why else would we have gone there?" Elizabeth asked, still managing to look quite innocent. "Someone has to help Cody. And if it's not going to be you—" her mother paused to sniff delicately "—well then, I guess it's just going to have to be me."

Maggy rolled her eyes toward the heavens. Her mother's performance was worthy of an award, but this time it wasn't going to work.

"Mother," Maggy said, trying to hide the smile that was threatening to break loose. "Cody is a big boy. I really don't think he needs our help."

Her mother perked up. "Well, dear, of course he does!"

"Now Maggy," Cody said, sliding his arm across the back of the couch behind her and giving her shoulder a pat. "I had no intention of coming here to make trouble between you and your mother. I agreed to take her to the club only because she wanted to see it. You yourself said she hasn't been out since your father—well, in a long time. I didn't see any harm in taking her somewhere I knew she'd enjoy herself.'' Cody gave her an impish grin. "We really did have a good time. Didn't we, Elizabeth?'' His eyes twinkled with delight, and Maggy turned to stare at him. Her suspicions grew; her mother and Cody *were* feathered from the same flock. All the more reason to stay away from the man!

"But you got arrested!'' Maggy cried incredulously, causing her mother to snort.

"Minor detail, dear. Minor detail. We could have outrun the cops,'' Elizabeth insisted. "And we wouldn't have gotten caught if I could have got my leg up over that brick wall. But my dress—'' Elizabeth stopped abruptly as she caught the stunned look on Maggy's face.

"Mother,'' Maggy said carefully. "Why were you trying to climb over a brick wall?''

"I think I'll go to bed,'' Elizabeth said abruptly, jumping to her feet.

"Mother,'' Maggy said sternly, unwilling to let her mother off the hook so easily. "I'm not done talking to you.''

Elizabeth deliberately ignored her. "Good night, dear,'' she said, bending to kiss Maggy's cheek. "I'll see you in the morning.'' Elizabeth moved toward Cody. "Thank you,'' she whispered, her eyes twinkling. "I don't know when I've had such a good time." Her words brought a soft chuckle from Cody, who sobered instantly at the look Maggy gave him.

"And I'm not finished with you, either," Maggy warned Cody, just in case he had any ideas of getting up and waltzing off without letting her have her say.

Cody's brows rose and he gave her a devilish smile that sent her pulse racing. "Good," he said, gently touching her cheek. "Because I'm not finished with you, either."

Now what was that supposed to mean? Maggy wondered with a frown, deliberately avoiding his gaze. His implication was clear, and Maggy realized if she had any sense she would head for the door. His words lay between them, full of promise. If Cody was trying to distract her from her anger, he had done a good job. He was looking at her in a way that made her feel very self-conscious, and very aware of him as a man.

Through the screen of her lashes, Maggy could see Cody's strong profile and lean features. She felt his eyes caress her, causing her anger to crumble like an overbaked cookie. Maggy heaved a soft sigh. Oh, how this man could complicate her life! No, her mind corrected. How this man *was* complicating her life.

She and Cody were two different people, Maggy rationalized. Cody was in love with life and wanted to sample and savor all the pleasures life had to offer, without having to worry about whether his actions were rational, logical or even sensible. Tonight was a perfect example. He gave no thought to the consequences of going to the Boom Boom Club. He only thought of the pleasure it would give her mother. Cody clearly played by his own rules—just like her mother.

Maggy glanced at him. How would he love? she wondered, shocked at the train of her thoughts. The answer came instantly. By his own rules, no doubt, just like he did everything else. Judging by his affection for Bobby, Cody's loving would probably be total and thorough. The thought sent a ripple of longing through her, and Maggy shivered.

Cody was so close she could see the thick sweep of dark lashes that circled his eyes. See the full softness of his mouth. A mouth that laughed too easily, and too often. For an instant, she wondered if his lips would feel as soft as they looked. Startled at her thoughts, she shook her head.

She couldn't allow herself to get involved with him, at least not personally involved. She couldn't afford to let her personal feelings grow.

Despite their differences and despite her resolve, Maggy realized she was far too attracted to the man for her own good. It was just that he was so blasted appealing! He seemed to be attacking her—however unconsciously—on all levels.

Physically, he was so attractive that he caused every one of her nerve endings to cry out with curiosity.

Emotionally, Cody appealed to the compassionate nature in her. She couldn't help but appreciate and admire the kind of man he was. To take on the responsibility of a child and raise him as his own, how could she find fault with him for that? Bobby was growing up in a secure, warm environment, full of love and devotion because of Cody.

Intellectually, Cody appealed to her reasonable, rational side. What he was trying to do, regardless of how bizarre it was, was noble and endearing. He was willing to risk his career just to insure Bobby's future. How on earth could she find fault with that?

She couldn't, Maggy realized dismally. And she knew it. It left her feeling so vulnerable.

"Mags?" Lost in her own thoughts, she jumped at the sound of his voice. Cody was so close that his soft breath teased her delicate skin. Startled, Maggy turned, and found him only inches away. Her breath lodged in the back of her throat like a broken chicken bone.

"What?" she stammered, allowing her eyes the pleasure of looking at him.

He was smiling down at her with such tenderness her stomach contracted. He dropped his fingers to her shoulders and traced a lazy pattern. Maggy squirmed uncomfortably. His touch was causing her breath to come quickly. If he was trying to distract her from their conversation, he was doing a good job. Struggling to attend to the matter at hand, Maggy shifted away, trying to get some relief from the heat radiating through her.

She had to handle this right here and now, or before she knew it, she would end up painting the jail, storming Washington or doing the Lord knew what else.

"I want to talk to you about my mother," Maggy finally said, forcing her mind back on track.

"Would it help if I said I was sorry about tonight?" He vainly tried to hide a smile, and Maggy looked at him dubiously.

"Are you sorry?" she inquired with a lift of her brow.

"Nope," he returned, grinning from ear to ear. "Your mother and I had a fine old time. You should have seen her, she was wonderful. I really think she had a good time. For a few moments there she forgot about everything. She was alive, Mags, and you heard her, she said she couldn't remember when she'd had so much fun. You know your mother. She's not happy unless she's got a cause to support, or someone to help. How can you be mad at her for that?"

She couldn't, Maggy realized with a scowl. "I thought you said you never did anything sensible or rational,'' she grumbled, and he laughed softly, giving her a quick hug.

"I guess even I do something surprising once in a while.''

Surprising? That sure was a funny name for what he was doing, Maggy decided. "Cody, you know all the reasons why I can't help you find a woman. We've already gone through it. You know what I think you should do.''

He nodded. "I know. You think I should do something sensible, rational, or—I forget the other one,'' he admitted with a lopsided grin.

"Logical,'' she managed to get out. "What you want to do isn't any of those things.'' She took a deep breath, hoping to calm her jagged nerves. "On the other hand,'' Maggy said carefully, "I don't want my mother traipsing around town trying to find a woman for you. Lord knows how much trouble she'll get into.'' Maggy failed to add that her mother left to her own devices was bad enough, but add Cody to the pot and she was certain the cauldron would be brewing with more trouble than even *she* could handle. There really was only one solution to the problem.

"I don't have any other choice but to help you myself,'' Maggy said glumly. His eyes were soft and warm and Maggy felt her stomach drop. "I'll help you find a woman,'' she stammered, dragging her eyes away from his in an effort to keep her mind on the problem at hand. At least if she handled it, if she helped him herself, she'd be able to have some control over the situation. And him. And her mother. Well, one could always hope.

"But I want you to know, Cody, I still don't like it." She tried to keep her voice firm, but made the mistake of looking directly into his eyes. A great fountain of warmth unleashed itself inside her. Those blue eyes, she thought hazily. Those beautiful blue eyes were going to be her downfall.

"I do appreciate it," he said tenderly, giving her shoulder a gentle squeeze and in the process pulling her closer so that one whole side of her body was pressed against him. She tried to draw back, but he wouldn't let her. "Hey, where are you going? Aren't you comfortable?"

Maybe he was comfortable, but for her, "comfortable" wasn't exactly the word that applied. Being so close to him was stirring up emotions and desires that were confusing. She wanted to stay near him, to feel the warmth of his body, the lazy touch of his hand. And yet by doing so she was creating an emotional volcano for herself.

"I'm comfortable," she mumbled, deliberately dropping her gaze to her lap so she wouldn't have to look at him. She tried to remember what she wanted to talk to him about, but all she could think about was his nearness. And what it was doing to her.

"Maggy?"

She took a small breath, knowing that was all she could manage in her present position. Instinct told her to move away from him, but emotions told her to stay. Emotions won.

"What?" she said quietly, picking at an imaginary speck on her skirt.

"I never properly thanked you for bailing me out. I really do appreciate it. And don't worry about your money. I don't have much cash on me, but I'll be happy to write you a check, or if you'd rather, I can transfer some money from my bank down home, but it will take a few days."

She turned to look at him. How on earth could he sit there carrying on about money and banks, when all she could do was think about his nearness? His eyes prowled her face, tenderly caressing every inch until she swallowed heavily.

"Mags?"

She watched a tiny pulse beat in his neck. "What?" she whispered.

"You're afraid of me, aren't you?" His fingers traced a lazy pattern along her arm.

"Of course not," she lied, unable to drag her eyes from his.

"You're afraid I'm going to be trouble, aren't you?"

Maggy sighed heavily. "Cody, you're already trouble."

The corners of his mouth lifted, and Maggy found herself answering his smile. The man *was* trouble, but Maggy had a sneaky feeling she was the one who was *in* trouble.

"You got that part right," he assured her, his eyes brimming with amusement. "But, honey, I always have fun."

Maggy nodded, feeling unaccountably flustered. She had to admit, he did seem to be having fun. He always seemed to be smiling, his eyes always seemed to be brimming with laughter. But what about the consequences of his fun? Like her mother, he rarely gave any thought to the consequences of his actions.

"Mags, remember when I told you I've never done a logical thing in my life?" She could only manage a nod, wondering just where this conversation was leading. "Well, never let it be said that I lied."

Maggy watched mesmerized as his face drew nearer. He was going to kiss her, and she knew it. Perhaps she should protest, she thought wildly, watching as his lips drew nearer in slow motion. But then Maggy realized she didn't want to protest, it was what she had been waiting for, what she had been anticipating from the moment she'd laid eyes on him.

Her breath lodged somewhere in her throat, and her body surged with sweet anticipation as his lips gently touched hers. His mouth was warm, softer than she'd imagined, sweeter than she'd ever dreamed. Her breath came at an uneven pace now as Cody's tongue gently tapped at her lips, urging her, encouraging her to allow him to explore. Maggy turned toward him, slipping her arms around him in welcome.

Her action caused Cody to growl softly, the sound rumbling up his chest as his arms embraced her. His hands slid up and down the length of her spine, touching, exploring, experiencing. Trembling, Maggy leaned into him, feeling the heat of his chest, the rapid pulse of his heart warm her breasts.

His lips gentled on hers as his tongue thoroughly sampled the silky warmth of her mouth. Cody tasted sweet, and dangerous. Ignoring the voice of reason that tried to caution her, Maggy ran her hands through the softness of his hair, wanting to feel every inch of him, wanting to experience everything he had to offer.

His hands roamed freely, so big, and yet so gentle as they spanned her slender waist, then moved upward to tease her rib cage.

Maggy moved her hands across his broad shoulders, enjoying the feel of his hard muscles against her soft palms. His kiss deepened, his lips sipping at hers until she was intoxicated with desire, drunk with unfamiliar longings.

Cody trailed his fingers slowly upward until they

tangled in her hair, urging her closer until there wasn't even room for a breath of air between them. Her heart slammed against her ribs as unfulfilled emotions stormed her body.

Whispering her name against her lips, Cody reluctantly rolled his mouth from hers. Cradling her face gently in his hands, he looked deep into her eyes.

"Oh honey," he whispered, scattering a rainbow of tiny kisses across her face. She closed her eyes and allowed herself the pleasure of his lips. Her mouth ached with longing, wanting to reacquaint itself with his.

Finally, Cody pressed his forehead against hers. "Mags," he said huskily, trying to talk around the catch in his throat. "I think I'd better say goodnight. While I still can," he added. His eyes were darkened by desire, and she could see a smattering of her lipstick on one corner of his mouth. Hesitantly Maggy lifted her hand and gently wiped it off. Cody caught her hand. His eyes pinned hers as he slowly brushed his warm mouth across the tender skin of her palm, sending a shiver of desire rippling through her. Stunned at the emotions that were ravaging her, Maggy pulled her hand free, embarrassed at the way she had responded to the man.

After dropping a quick kiss on her forehead, Cody rose. "Thank you for everything, honey, and for agreeing to help me despite how you feel about it.

That takes a lot of courage, and I admire that." He turned and scooped Bobby off the couch. "Tomorrow, well—tomorrow we'll talk some more." He grinned and flashed her a wink. "Your mother and I have some ideas for you."

Maggy nodded, still in a daze. Tomorrow she would have to try to figure out exactly what had happened tonight.

She lifted a finger to her lips and her eyes closed as she remembered the taste of him. A thought penetrated her hazy brain and her eyes opened as she jerked upright.

They had conned her! Cody and her mother had known all along she was going to help him! They'd somehow managed to cajole and confuse her into agreeing to do just what they wanted!

Maggy smiled in spite of herself. Handling her mother wasn't easy, but handling her mother and Cody was going to be... Oh Lord, what on earth had she gotten herself into?

Another thought crept slowly into her mind and a skitter of anxiety tensed her frame. Just what on earth did Cody mean—they had some ideas for her? Just what kind of ideas?

Maggy groaned softly. Knowing her mother and Cody, even tarring and feathering couldn't be ruled out!

Chapter Five

"Come on, tiger, eat your breakfast." Cody's voice filtered through the lower level of the house, and Maggy quickened her footsteps in time with her pulse rate. Despite her misgivings, just knowing Cody was downstairs caused her to smile.

"Come on, tiger, just a little bit more. That's a good boy. No, it doesn't go on your head. No, don't spit—Bobby!"

Maggy stepped into the kitchen and burst out laughing. Cody was vainly trying to wipe puddled milk and cereal off his face.

"Good morning," she said, trying not to laugh at the scowl on Cody's face or the cereal in his hair. "What are you two up to?" she asked with a smile.

A dish towel was thrown carelessly over Cody's

bare shoulder and he lifted one corner to mop his face. "I'm trying to give him his breakfast," Cody grumbled. "And he's trying to give it back to me. I think we're at a standoff." He glanced up at Maggy and grinned. "Don't you look lovely this morning?" Cody's gaze slowly went over her, taking her in from head to toe. His eyes gently slid over the pale blue linen suit, with its matching silk blouse. She had pulled her hair up into a chignon, letting tiny wisps curl at her ears.

Self-consciously Maggy lifted a shaky hand to touch her hair. When Cody looked at her like that she felt warm all over. The man could do things to her just with his eyes that—

"Ma-ma!" Bobby squealed, drawing her attention. The toddler looked at her with such total adoration that Maggy's heart melted.

"Morning, Sport," she whispered, leaning down to plant a soft kiss on the toddler's cheek. He smelled clean and sweet and totally irresistible. Bobby beamed up at her and Maggy slid a hand across his head, ruffling his hair. Cody was watching her intently, a quiet smile on his face.

"Where's my mother?" Maggy inquired, unsettled now because of the way the man was looking at her.

"Sleeping," Cody returned.

"Ma-ma, eat?" Bobby asked, turning big pleading eyes on her. No longer surprised at his expressions of endearment, Maggy smiled, feeling all her maternal instincts reach out to the motherless child.

"Eat!" Bobby insisted, reaching out to tug on her arm with a slightly damp hand. Maggy glanced down at her watch and frowned. She had overslept this morning, and was now running late. Miss Barklay was absolutely passionate about punctuality. But still—Maggy looked at Bobby. His big blue eyes were fixed on her in a way that tore at her heart. He'd had so little maternal affection or attention, no wonder he responded so warmly and quickly to her. How could she turn her back on him? She was torn between staying and feeding him, which she really wanted to do—or getting to work on time—which she knew she really *should* do.

"Not now, tiger," Cody admonished gently, peeling the child's hand from Maggy's arm. "Maggy has to get to work."

"Ma-ma, eat!" Bobby demanded, kicking his chubby feet against the chair. His lips formed a quivering pout as tears welled up in his eyes; a giant tear plopped down his face and rolled slowly down his cheek.

That did it! Maggy yanked off her jacket and draped it across the back of a chair.

She was already late, she was going to get a lecture from Miss Barklay whether she was an hour late, or over two, so a few more minutes wouldn't matter. At the moment, comforting Bobby was up-permost in her mind.

"It's all right, Cody," Maggy said. "I'll stay."

Cody stood up.

And Maggy sat down.

"Something wrong, Mags?" Cody asked with a twinkle in his eye. He cocked his head and watched as a slow flush crept over her pale features. She tried to look everywhere but at him. But her traitorous eyes kept going back to him.

Wrong? Maggy swallowed hard. What could pos-sibly be wrong? Just because there was a gorgeous nearly naked man standing in her kitchen, what could possibly be wrong?

Cody was dressed in a pair of ragged cutoffs— and nothing else. His feet were as bare as his chest. At least he had told her the truth about not liking clothes, she mused humorously, trying not to stare at the magnificence of his body.

A shaft of lemon-colored sunlight filtered through the corner window, highlighting Cody's bronzed chest. His stomach, she noted, was flat and narrow, and his navel peeked out atop the waistband of his shorts.

Maggy tried not to stare at him. She was both excited and aggravated...aggravated that she found him so exciting!

She was supposed to be there for Bobby, Maggy

chastised herself, not drooling over Cody like one of Miss Avalon's schoolgirls.

"Want some coffee?" Cody inquired. "I just made it." Maggy nodded, dragging her eyes from his and pouring all her concentration into the oat cereal, which Bobby was trying to spoon into his mouth. Cody leaned over and slowly slid a steaming cup of coffee in front of her. His muscles contracted with each movement, and she watched mesmerized.

Her pulse throbbed at the back of her throat as his arm brushed against hers. Tremors ran a wild race, chasing each other up and down her spine. Every time the man came near, she felt as if she were airborne—without a plane.

What on earth was wrong with her?

Last night she had lain awake for hours, thinking about Cody, about his kisses and her reactions to them. Never had she reacted so boldly, so wantonly to a man. Not that there had ever been a man in her life. Other than colleagues from the academy and a few casual dates, Maggy was inexperienced in the matter of men. Cody was unlike any man she'd ever met. Despite her reservations, Maggy found herself drawn to him and haunted by him.

It had been nearly dawn before she'd fallen asleep, with the image of Cody firmly planted in her jumbled mind. Last night she had realized that even though Cody was just down the hall, there was a great deal more than just a couple of walls separating them. *A great deal more.*

She'd do well to remember that, Maggy lectured herself, but it was hard to remember anything this morning with Cody here, large as life, looking more appealing than any man had a right to.

"Done," Bobby announced, spitting a stream of cereal in her direction. Maggy jumped back and uttered a wild screech as cereal pelted her blouse and face.

"Tiger!" Cody growled. "Look what you did! You got cereal all over Maggy."

"All done, Da-da," Bobby repeated with a grin as he pushed the bowl of cereal perilously close to the edge of the table.

Grabbing the bowl just before it went sailing through the air, Cody yanked the towel off his shoulder and dabbed at the front of Maggy's blouse. Her eyes closed as her body quaked at his touch. Swallowing hard, she tried to gather her composure. Having Cody's hands on such an intimate part of her body caused her blood to zip wildly through her veins. She glanced down at his hand and her breathing came quickly as her heart danced a wicked dance.

"I...I can do that, Cody," she stammered, raising a shaky hand to take the towel from him.

"I know," Cody said cheerfully, his eyes alight with mischief. "But it's more fun if I do it."

Her startled eyes flew to his and she saw the wicked amusement spreading across his features. He was having fun with her again, Maggy realized. He was trying to keep her off balance with his outrageousness and, she thought mildly, he was doing a good job of it. Why did she have the feeling that she was mired ankle deep in quicksand and sinking fast?

"I've got to get to work," she announced shakily, grabbing her jacket off the back of the chair. "See you later, Sport." She leaned down and kissed Bobby's cheek. He responded with a toothy grin. "Be good," she added with a laugh, ruffling his hair.

"What about me?" Cody inquired with a devilish smile as he scooped up Bobby. He paused to wipe Bobby's hands before plopping the squirming toddler securely on his hip. "Don't you want me to be good, too?" Cody inquired, his eyes still twinkling with mischief. Maggy rolled her eyes toward the heavens. If Cody's escapade with her mother last night was an indication of his idea of "being good," she wasn't certain she could handle any more of it.

"I'd settle for staying out of trouble," Maggy muttered under her breath as she slipped her arms into her jacket sleeves.

"Maggy," Cody said, trying to help her into her jacket, despite the fact that she didn't need his help. He dropped one big hand around her neck and pulled her close. She could feel the warmth of his body. "I can stay out of trouble *and* be good. In fact," he said, lowering his voice and flashing her a wink, "I can be *very* good."

Her face flamed at the double meaning of his words and she stepped away from him. She had no doubt Cody would be good, *very* good at whatever he chose to do. She just hoped he could be very good at staying out of trouble, for the time being, anyway.

"Now," Cody went on, resting his hand on the middle of her back as he ushered her toward the door. "Off to work. When you get home, I'll have a surprise for you."

"A surprise?" Maggy came to an abrupt halt and looked up at him. Cody looked much too mischievous for her peace of mind. "What kind of surprise?" she asked hesitantly, trying not to let her fear show. She didn't know if she could take any more of Cody's surprises.

"Mags," he said, sounding clearly affronted. "Don't you trust me?"

"No," she returned, and Cody grinned.

"Now don't you worry," he said in a tone of voice that caused her to do just that. "I've got some ideas for you." Cody stopped at the telephone table to scoop up several paperbacks. "Here's a couple of my books. I thought you might like to take a look at them." Cody pressed the books into her hands and opened the front door. "Bobby and I will keep things square here. Won't we, Sport?" Bobby grinned in response. "And don't worry about your mother, we'll keep an eye on her, too."

Yes, but who was going to keep an eye on him? Maggy wondered, lifting her hand to return Bobby's wave.

"Bye-bye, Ma-ma," Bobby called, waving a chubby fist at her.

"Bye, Sport." Maggy blew him a kiss.

"Mags, wait," Cody called, and she stood still again with a frown. Shielding her eyes against the harsh sunlight Maggy looked back at him.

"What's wrong?"

"You forgot something." Cody tried not to smile as Maggy checked her briefcase, her purse and the books he had given her. It appeared she had everything, but she obediently marched back up the walk to him.

"What did I forget?"

Cradling Bobby between them, Cody leaned forward. "You forgot to kiss *me* goodbye." Before she could open her mouth to protest, Cody's lips were on hers, draining her mind and her body of everything but the feel of him. With a sigh, she kissed him in return, realizing she could easily get used to starting the day this way. Cody rolled his lips from hers, and planted a playful kiss on her nose.

"Now off you go," he instructed as he turned her around and pointed her toward the driveway.

"See you tonight," Cody called as she walked away on shaky limbs. She turned back to wave and saw Cody's eyes crinkling in delight. It caused her heart to lurch unexpectedly. Another one of Cody's ideas, she thought again as she backed her car out of the driveway and headed toward the academy. She wasn't certain if she could stand any more surprises—or ideas. But her curiosity got the better of her, and she couldn't help but wonder just what Cody had in store. She only hoped that whatever it was, it wouldn't land them all in jail this time.

"Margaret!" Miss Barklay's shrill voice came out of nowhere and the book Maggy had been reading—Cody's book—went flying through the air.

"Miss Barklay," Maggy stammered nervously, trying to glance around and under her desk for her dropped book before her boss saw it. Maggy spotted the novel on the far side of her desk, almost touching the toe of Miss Barklay's sensible low-heeled oxfords. Deftly Maggy slid lower in her chair, stretching her leg as far as she could, trying to maneuver the book toward her with the toe of her shoe.

Somehow she had managed to avoid Miss Barklay all morning. But now, during her lunch hour, the woman had finally shown up. Miss Barklay was stationed in front of Maggy's desk, watching her perform ankle gymnastics in an effort to retrieve Cody's book.

"May I ask what you're doing?" Miss Barklay inquired with a frown, as Maggy tried to maneuver Cody's book out of range of her boss's piercing eyes.

"I dropped something," Maggy muttered, scooting lower in her chair. She could just about reach the book, if only she could scoot forward a little farther! Miss Barklay bent over and picked the book up from the floor.

"What's this?" One silver brow rose and Maggy groaned inwardly as Miss Barklay carefully examined Cody's book. A scantily clad woman with ample curves and cleavage adorned the elaborately decorated cover.

Miss Barklay's brows rose again, almost disappearing in the circle of white curls that marched obediently around her head. "Is this one of the books you confiscated from one of the students last semester?" Her voice was laced with displeasure and Maggy sat perfectly still, holding her breath as Miss Barklay flipped casually through the book. The woman's eyes widened occasionally as a certain passage caught her attention.

Miss Barklay's tongue clucked in disapproval. "This is deplorable!" she announced with a heavy sigh. "I swear, Margaret, one never knows what young ladies will do next. We've tried to instill good values and morals, and then, just when I'm certain they've learned the proper reading—''

"It's mine," Maggy said weakly.

Miss Barklay's eyes widened in surprise. "I beg your pardon?" she said stiffly.

"It's...mine. The book is mine," Maggy repeated, feeling her face flame.

"*You*'re reading *Wild Bill Cody's Amazing Adventures of the Amazon*?" Miss Barklay looked at Maggy as if her IQ had suddenly dropped to double digits. Sinking deeper in her chair, Maggy offered her boss a weak smile.

"Margaret," Miss Barklay said carefully, her tone of voice low and controlled. "I don't believe this title—or this subject matter—was on the recommended reading list for this semester." She did not try to hide her contempt.

"No, it's not," Maggy returned, pulling herself up once more and meeting the headmistress's frosty gaze. "The author—the author is a friend of mine."

Her employer's body stiffened, and she glared at Maggy from beneath a shelf of fuzzy white brows. "You're *acquainted* with a person named Wild Bill Cody?"

Never had Maggy heard such a harmless word sound so ominous. Miss Barklay made *acquainted* sound like some bawdy, indecent cult ritual. Why on earth should she feel guilty? Maggy wondered. It was *her* lunch hour, and *her* time, she thought defiantly, not to mention *her* book. So what difference did it make to Miss Barklay what she read? Judging from the look on the woman's face, it did make a difference.

"Yes, as a matter of fact I am," Maggy admitted reluctantly, meeting her boss's disapproving gaze.

"I see."

From the expression on her face, Maggy knew that Miss Barklay didn't see—not at all. Maggy felt a rare and sudden flare of rebellion.

What did her acquaintances have to do with her capabilities as an administrator? Maggy asked herself dismally. Or with her possible future as headmistress? How she conducted her private life and with whom should be just that, *private*.

But, Maggy realized sadly, it wasn't. Her life, all aspects of it, had to meet Miss Barklay's strict standards. Her actions at all times must be totally above reproach. Maggy had been well aware of this when she accepted her present position.

She had always felt comfortable and secure living her life within the structured boundaries laid down by Miss Barklay. The high standards and restrictions had never bothered her. Until now. Until Cody had burst into her life.

While she loved her job, and loved working with children, Maggy had to admit that this was one time she wished her position didn't require such regimented behavior.

Maggy couldn't help but wonder how her boss would react if she knew just *how* acquainted she was with Cody. Sighing, Maggy dreamily remembered the touch of his lips on hers that morning as he'd kissed her goodbye. She felt an inexplicable pang of loneliness well up inside her.

"Margaret!" Maggy's eyes flew open, and she flushed. "I don't think I need to remind you that the staff of Miss Avalon's must be of the highest moral— My dear, what on earth is in your hair?"

"My hair?" Maggy repeated blankly as Miss Barklay leaned over and plucked something from her shiny blond locks. Maggy swallowed hard. The items in Miss Barklay's hand looked suspiciously like...Bobby's breakfast. Oh Lord!

"Is this cereal?" Miss Barklay inquired, staring at the little round oats lying in her hand. The cereal reminded Maggy of Bobby, and she felt another pang as she thought of the chubby-cheeked cherub who had suddenly claimed her as his own.

"Margaret," Miss Barklay said carefully. "I don't suppose you'd care to explain why you're adorning your hair with cereal?" One brow rose and Maggy shrugged helplessly. There was no way she could explain to Miss Barklay *why* she was reading *Adventures of the Amazon* or wearing oat cereal in her hair, or even why she was acquainted with a person named *Wild Bill Cody*. She wasn't even tempted to try.

Scowling, Miss Barklay dusted the oats off her hand as if they were going to sprout antennae and attack. "Margaret," she began slowly. "I came in here to discuss several matters with you. None of which was your choice of reading material or hair adornment." Miss Barklay inhaled deeply. "You were over an hour late for school this morning. Punctuality is not merely an exercise in courtesy. It's a form of discipline that must not be taken lightly. I trust this won't become a habitual occurrence?" Her tone of voice made the offense sound like treason. "Even though the students won't be arriving until next week, you know how important discipline is to one's life. Without discipline, life would be chaos."

Discipline. Yes, one had to have discipline in one's life, Maggy conceded. But what about a little room for fun and excitement as well? she wondered gloomily, shocked at her own thoughts.

"I'm sorry," Maggy said, trying to sound contrite. "I was—" Maggy hedged "—detained." Detained and reined in by a matched pair of charming men.

"Detained?" Miss Barklay repeated, clearly wanting more of an explanation than the one she'd been given. When none was forthcoming, she continued. "Now, for the other item," she said, her tone of voice indicating she had saved the worst for last. "Margaret, have you seen this morning's paper?"

Was this some kind of a test? Maggy wondered. "No, I'm sorry, I haven't had a chance to look at it." She'd been too engrossed in Cody's book to do anything.

As if reading her thoughts, Miss Barklay cast a baleful glance at the book in question. "Yes, well, I can see that you've been otherwise…engaged. On the front page of this morning's paper, there was an article regarding that disgraceful club on the out-skirts of town." Miss Barklay frowned and tapped a slim finger against her pale lips. "I can't seem to recall the name."

Maggy stiffened as familiar feelings of helpless-ness washed over her. She swallowed hard, knowing what was coming.

"The Boom Boom Club?" Maggy supplied dully.

"*You*'re acquainted with that establishment, too?" Miss Barklay's voice whistled out of her pursed lips. If being late was treason, being ac-quainted with the Boom Boom Club was clearly a lynching offense.

"No, not really," Maggy assured her quickly. "I've just…heard of it."

"Are you certain you've never been there?" Miss Barklay inquired suspiciously, clearly not believing her.

"I can assure you, Miss Barklay, that I have never been in the Boom Boom Club." Too bad she couldn't say the same about some other members of her family, Maggy thought, remembering her mother's escapades. She sobered immediately at Miss Barklay's frown.

"This morning's paper reported that a raid was held at that disgusting club last night. Apparently they have people who dance for money and then remove their clothing—"

"Strippers," Maggy supplied helpfully, immediately regretting her words at the look that contracted her boss's face.

"Strippers?" Miss Barklay shuddered. "Apparently several patrons as well as—" Maggy could see she couldn't bring herself to say the word "—as well as employees of that establishment were arrested last night. I understand that there was quite a fracas involving picketers and the police. Anyway, several people were arrested and detained at the jail. I was almost certain there was a Magee listed in the paper."

Maggy sobered instantly. She could see the position of headmistress slowly slipping out of her reach. She felt an unexpected tug of panic. This was what she had always feared—that one of her mother's escapades would cost her her job.

Maggy had worked so hard for this; it meant so much to her. Why, she wondered now, did Miss Barklay's rules about her personal life have to be so confining, so restricting? When she thought about it, what had happened to her mother and Cody really wasn't all that terrible. But she knew Miss Barklay would never see it that way.

"Miss Barklay," Maggy said firmly, coming to her feet. "I can assure you that I have never been to the Boom Boom Club, nor have I ever been arrested. Neither here," Maggy added for good measure at the look on Miss Barklay's face, "nor anywhere else." It wasn't a lie, Maggy rationalized. She had never been at the club, nor had she been arrested. On the other hand, it wasn't entirely the truth, either.

She probably should have confessed that the Magee in question was indeed a member of her family, but Maggy immediately felt an overwhelming sense of duty to protect her mother. Her mother didn't work at the school, nor did she have any responsibility to Miss Barklay. Besides, Maggy reasoned, why should her mother have to abide by Miss Barklay's rules and regulations?

What her mother did was of no concern to Miss Barklay. And, Maggy had to concede, despite her distress at the situation last night, it had all worked out for the best. If pressed, Maggy would have to admit that it did sound as though her mother and Cody had had fun. Now, in the light of day, she could almost see the humor in the situation. Almost. But she saw no reason to admit her mother's involvement to her boss. Miss Barklay would never understand.

"Well, if you're sure," Miss Barklay said finally, and Maggy sighed in relief, hoping her boss was going to let the matter drop. "You must realize how concerned I am. Something like that—well—how would it look if one of our staff were involved in something like that? It...it...would be deplorable."

"Deplorable," Maggy confirmed, nodding her head in agreement, and wondering all the while just what would be so deplorable about it!

"Well then, I believe that's all for now. I suggest you carry on with your work. There's much to do before the students begin arriving next week. I will be having my customary faculty tea three weeks from Friday. I trust you'll be there?"

Maggy almost groaned. Miss Barklay's faculty teas were the drudge of the year. They were held in Avalon Hall to welcome returning faculty as well as new staff members. They were stiff, boring, formal affairs where everyone walked around as if on eggs, scarcely breathing lest someone do something to displease Miss Barklay or catch her ever-watchful eye.

The competition among the staff to get in the woman's good graces was almost comical to watch. Perhaps it was because Maggy had never engaged in such trivial one-upmanship that Miss Barklay had singled her out to become her successor.

Well, Maggy reasoned, until this morning she *had* been singled out to be her successor. Now, looking at the woman's accusing gaze, she wasn't quite sure what her future held. Judging from her employer's demeanor, a psychiatric evaluation might be high on the list.

"I wouldn't miss it," Maggy lied, knowing she'd rather face a firing squad than have to endure another one of Miss Barklay's faculty teas.

"Very well, then. Carry on, Margaret." Miss Barklay reached down, picked up Cody's book off the desk and turned on her heel. Maggy felt a moment of panic. Whether her boss liked her choice in reading material or not, Cody had given the book to her, and it meant a lot to her. Maggy wanted it back.

"Miss Barklay?" Maggy's voice was tremulous. "May I have my book back, please?" Her words caused the other woman's feet to stop as if brakes had been applied to her rubber soles. Miss Barklay swiveled toward Maggy, hostility flickering in her eyes.

"Why on earth would you want this back?" she inquired curtly. "Surely you don't intend to continue reading this...this...trash?"

"Trash" was probably the word that did it. Maggy surged to her feet as anger coursed through her. She threw back her shoulders and met the older woman's gaze. For some crazy reason, Maggy was not about to back down on this issue.

"Miss Barklay," she said slowly. "That book is hardly trash. While it might not be on the recommended reading list for the students of Miss Avalon's Academy, I can assure you that it is a well-written, well-plotted story that I happen to have found very interesting. And not only did I find it interesting," Maggy went on, realizing she was probably digging her own grave. "But so have a great deal of other people. You'll see that on the cover the publisher has made reference to the fact that the series of books by this particular author has sold very well. In fact, most of them have been best-sellers."

"But surely—"

"May I have it back, please?" Maggy held out a shaky hand and waited. Miss Barklay's lips thinned in annoyance and for a moment stormy green eyes warred with cold blue ones. Finally, Miss Barklay slapped the book into Maggy's waiting hand, then turned on her heel and left Maggy's office.

"I expect you to be prompt at the faculty tea," Miss Barklay warned over her shoulder.

Clutching the book tightly to her breast, Maggy heaved a weary sigh of relief and slumped in her chair, feeling inexplicably proud of herself. She had stood toe-to-toe with Miss Barklay for the very first time, and to her surprise it made her feel very good.

She glanced down at the cover of Cody's book and smiled. Somehow she had a feeling that Wild Bill Cody had had a lot to do with her actions today. Whether she wanted to admit it or not, Maggy knew that Cody and his craziness were having an effect on her.

There was just something about the man. He was big and macho, yet despite all that there was something warm and vulnerable about him, something that made women want to reach out to him, to hold him in their arms.

The man made her head spin with his impulsive craziness, yet at the same time made her toes curl with his tenderness.

So why, Maggy asked herself, wasn't she running for cover?

Chapter Six

"You'd better lift your chin, honey, your face is so long it's scraping the sidewalk." Cody stood in the doorway, smiling as Maggy dragged herself up the walk. Her euphoria at standing up to Miss Barklay had dissolved into remorse, followed quickly by regret.

This afternoon she had done exactly what she had always accused her mother of doing—not thinking through the consequences of things.

Why on earth had she done such a thing? What on earth had ever possessed her to defy her boss like that? She had berated herself nonstop for her impulsive actions. But, she finally realized, no amount of sorrow could erase what was done. All she could do now was prevent any further lapses. And Maggy was determined to do that.

Well, she admitted glumly as she trudged up the walk, her determination was much stronger when she wasn't staring at Cody's wonderful face. Somehow the sight of him weakened her resolve.

Annoyed that the sight of him also immediately lifted her spirits, Maggy tried to stamp down the welcoming smile that was threatening her lips.

"Bad day?" he asked, dropping a hand to her shoulder and giving it an encouraging squeeze.

"The worst," she mumbled. His fingers gently kneaded her shoulders, easing away the tension. Her emotional battery had nearly been drained, but somehow his presence seemed to recharge her. And further annoyed her.

"Do you want to talk about it?" he asked quietly, as if sensing her distress. Maggy looked up at him. Oh, how she longed to talk to him, to confide in him all the confusing emotions she was feeling. His shoulder looked so warm and inviting, just the place to lean her weary head and pour out her troubles. But Maggy knew she couldn't afford such a luxury. She had to keep Cody at a distance, for the sake and sanity of her health. And her heart.

Cody's gaze sought hers and for a moment his eyes seemed to be sending a silent message that only she could read. It frightened her with its intensity.

"Well," she said slowly, "to begin with I was an

hour late for school this morning. Then I got caught reading—'' Maggy stopped abruptly, wondering if Cody's feelings would be hurt if she told him the whole story, and decided it wasn't worth finding out.

"You got caught reading what?" He took her briefcase from her hand and dropped an arm around her shoulders.

"Nothing," she stammered, letting him lead her into the house.

"Ma-ma!" Bobby's eyes lit up when he saw Maggy, and her heart melted. Dressed only in a diaper, Bobby was sitting in the middle of the living room playing with some toys. The toddler struggled to his feet, holding on to the table for support. Delighted at the sight of his chubby, cheerful face, Maggy bent down and held out her arms to him. Taking awkward steps, Bobby moved quickly to her.

Scooping him up in her arms, Maggy laughed softly and swung him around and around.

"More!" Bobby gurgled, trying to squirm free. Maggy hugged him close, burying her face in his neck and cuddling the soft folds until he was giggling helplessly.

"Did you miss me, Sport?" she crooned, planting a bouquet of kisses across his cheek. Bobby wiggled impatiently as she held him tight, inhaling his sweet baby smell. Holding him close seemed to ease her despair. This little child had wormed his way quickly and quietly into her fragile heart.

"Miss Sport," he mimicked, and Maggy planted another fat kiss on the baby's cheek, not realizing until this moment just how much she had missed him.

Or Cody, she thought, glancing up. With a tinge of disappointment Maggy realized he was fully dressed. She was getting kind of used to seeing his naked chest. But his clothing only emphasized his masculinity. Dark slacks hugged his slim hips and covered his long legs like a second skin. His shirt, left open at the collar, only accentuated the broad expanse of his shoulders and chest. The sleeves were rolled up, revealing a dusty trail of dark hair.

Cody stood there watching her, holding her briefcase in his hand as if he had forgotten it was there. His eyes were warm and caring, and not just for Bobby, she realized suddenly, but for her as well. Lord, she was sinking deeper and deeper and somehow she didn't seem to have the willpower to help herself. Fearing Cody might read her thoughts, Maggy glanced away self-consciously, planting another kiss on Bobby's cheek.

"Don't I get one of those?" Cody asked, flashing her a warm smile. Maggy looked away. Oh, how she wanted to kiss him, to hold him in her arms the way she had done with Bobby! But she was determined both to keep out of Cody's arms and keep him out of her heart. Cody's kisses and caresses had muddled her brain and muddied her senses, and Maggy knew she simply couldn't allow it anymore.

She was going to do what she had promised, help him find a woman, and then send him on his way so that her life could get back to normal. Although Maggy wasn't certain she knew exactly what *normal* was anymore. Was it Miss Barklay's rigid rules and regulations? Or Cody's devil-may-care craziness? She didn't know, and right now she was too tired to think about it.

Banishing such thoughts, Maggy turned and flashed him what she hoped was a bright smile.

"What?" she inquired, deliberately not understanding.

"What?" he echoed, dropping her briefcase on the floor and crossing the room to stand just a breath away from her. "A kiss." His words caused her heart to flutter wildly in her breast. His gaze caressed her face, going over every one of her features. Maggy swallowed hard. "Bobby's not the only one who missed you. *I* missed you, too," Cody said, lifting a hand to her cheek. Her heart slowly unfolded, reaching out to him.

Maggy glanced up at Cody and without thinking she leaned toward him, lifting her face for his kiss. His lips were warm and moist, and he tasted faintly of lemonade.

"Down!" Wiggling and squirming, Bobby started

to protest. Reluctantly Maggy dragged her mouth from Cody's.

"Here you two are," Elizabeth said, sweeping into the room. Blinking, Maggy looked at her mother and shook her head. Today Elizabeth wore an elaborate silk dress that knotted over one shoulder and bared the other. A dime-store necklace of assorted colored pop beads circled her slender neck, while mismatched diamond earrings hung heavily from her ears. On her feet she wore bright green running shoes that Maggy knew for a fact glowed in the dark.

"That's some outfit, Mother," Maggy commented with a laugh.

Elizabeth glanced down at herself then twirled around, holding the skirt aloft. "Isn't it though, dear! I rather like it myself." She scooped Bobby from Maggy's arms. "Kiss dada good-night," Elizabeth ordered, waiting while Bobby kissed first Cody, and then Maggy. "Now, if you'll excuse us, we have a date."

"A date!" Maggy looked at her mother suspiciously. "What kind of a date?"

"With a greasy hamburger," Elizabeth replied, heading for the door.

"Mother," Maggy protested. "You can't take Bobby out like that! He only has a diaper on. You can't parade around town with him dressed like that!"

"I'm dressed enough for both of us. Besides, it's hotter than blazes outside. The child's comfortable just as he is."

Her mother had a point. It was blisteringly hot outside, and Bobby did look comfortable. But Maggy wasn't about to give in so easily. She didn't know what her mother was up to, but she had a feeling it was no good. "You can't feed that child greasy food, either," Maggy said, hoping to stall her mother's departure until she found out exactly what she was planning.

"And why not?" her mother inquired, coming to a halt and swiveling her head in Maggy's direction. "Half the country's population has grown up on fast food. Besides, Bobby likes hamburgers, don't you, sweetie?"

"Burgers!" Bobby demanded with a hopeful grin and Elizabeth smiled.

"See," she said, flashing Maggy a triumphant look. Maggy glanced at Cody for some help. He just shrugged his shoulders and grinned in his turn.

"Besides, dear," Elizabeth said, inching toward the door. "We're not just going for hamburgers. Are we, Sport?"

"What do you mean, you're not just going for hamburgers?" Maggy asked suspiciously, clearly not liking the sound of this.

"I told you, but you weren't listening. You never listen to me anymore," her mother complained, inching closer and closer toward the front door. "We have a date, don't we, Sport? We're going to meet the mayor."

"You're what!" Maggy started toward her mother, but Cody grabbed her arm and stopped her. She could feel the warmth of his fingers even through the fabric of her suit. It distracted her momentarily.

"Mother," Maggy called, watching helplessly as her mother snuck out the door. "What are you meeting the mayor about?"

"Don't get excited, dear," her mother called back. "It's nothing for you to worry about. I'm only going to talk to the mayor about the dreadful condition of the penal facilities in this state. We're going to persuade him to redecorate the jail. Aren't we, Sport?"

"Oh my God," Maggy whimpered. "Mother!" she called frantically, feeling the pendulum of doom swing closer. "Mother!" When there was no answer, Maggy whirled on Cody. "Say something!"

Cody looked at her quizzically for a moment, then crossed to the open door in two long strides with Maggy on his heels.

"Have a good time, Elizabeth. And Bobby only likes ketchup on his burgers—ouch, Mags, what'd you hit me for?" Rubbing his arm, and grinning from ear to ear, Cody looked down at her.

"That's not what I meant," she hissed, giving

him another whack on the arm. If Cody and her mother were having a race to see who would be the first to drive her crazy, they were in a dead heat!

Cody grinned at her harassed expression. "Now come on, Mags, it's not so bad. The mayor will probably love your mother." He looped an arm around her shoulder, but Maggy stepped out of his embrace. He was not going to drown her in his charm this time, she resolved firmly, shoring up her defenses.

"Mother!" she yelled, trying to go out the door after her. Cody grabbed the back of her suit and held on tight. "I'm not bailing you out this time," she called, twisting and trying to get free. Her mother's soft chuckle filtered through the night.

"That's all right," Elizabeth caroled merrily. "Cody will."

Maggy turned on him. Fury darkened her eyes. "You knew about this, didn't you?" she accused him and he had the audacity to grin. "How could you let her just walk out of here?" Maggy cried. "You knew what she was up to, and you didn't even try to stop her!"

"Stop her?" Cody looked totally bewildered. "Why should I try to stop her? She's a grown woman, Mags, and besides," he added with an infuriating grin, "Bobby *does* like burgers."

"Ahgggg!" Maggy growled, throwing up her hands in despair. She should have known better than to expect any help from him. "Do you have any idea what the mayor is going to do when he gets a gander at my mother and her little proposition? After what happened last night, Cody, I can't believe you just let her waltz out of here—and what about Bobby?" she demanded, abruptly changing stride. "That child should not be wandering around town only in a diaper, not to mention eating fast—"

"Mags?" he said softly, dropping his hands to her shoulders again and stopping her tirade. She looked up at him, her eyes meeting his until her legs grew weak.

"What!" she yelled, trying to pretend that his nearness wasn't affecting her.

"Are you upset?" he asked, grinning crookedly and looking down at her harassed expression. Maggy swore softly and turned away from him. The man was impossible, and, she thought morosely, he was going to drive her crazy. If she wasn't already crazy.

"Ready to hear my idea now?" Cody whispered suddenly to the back of her ear because she wouldn't turn to face him. She could feel his warm breath tickle her neck and despite herself, Maggy found herself smiling. Cody's cologne tonight was different, she thought hazily, potent and tantalizing, drugging her senses into a warm lethargy. He was infatuating and exasperating, and he was trying to drown her in his charm again. But it wasn't going to work.

Maggy swallowed hard. Well, one could only hope it wasn't going to work. Judging from the wicked pounding of her heart, Maggy wasn't so sure.

"Do I have a choice in the matter?" she muttered, turning around despite his closeness.

"Nope," he assured her.

"Let's hear it, then." Maggy heaved a heavy sigh and tried to prepare herself for what was to come.

Cody suddenly frowned, his dark brows drawing together as his eyes went over her. "You'll have to change," he announced abruptly, grabbing her elbow and hustling her toward the stairs. Maggy dug her heels in.

"*That*'s your idea?" she cried, wondering what kind of craziness he was trying to drag her into now. "I have to change? What kind of an idea is that?"

"No, no, no." He laughed, pulling her along and urging her up the steps. "My idea is where *we*'re going, not what you're wearing. But you'll have to change before we can get where we're going." He flashed her a wicked smile as if what he was saying made perfect sense.

"Cody." She sighed, shaking her head slowly. "What you just said made absolutely no sense."

His grin widened. "I know. It wasn't supposed to. I'm the one who never does anything sensible, reasonable or..." He frowned.

"Rational," she supplied, moving up the steps now, despite the fact that she didn't know what to

wear or where they were going. But she did know
that she was going to go along with him, *wherever*
it was they were going. At the top of the stairs she
turned back to look at him. "Cody?"

"What?" He was looking up at her, his arms
crossed, and a wide smile split his face.

"This isn't going to get us arrested, is it?" she
inquired with some concern. His smile grew wider,
and so did her concern.

"Now would I do something like that?" he asked,
managing to look quite innocent.

"Probably," Maggy said, trying not to laugh.

"Could we have a little trust here?"

"Trust, after that little speech you just gave?"
One brow rose and Maggy stared down at him, deciding to play along with him despite, or maybe because of the kind of day she'd had. Her despair had
lifted in the past few minutes.

"Why are you looking at me like that?" he inquired, and Maggy frowned.

"Like what?"

His mouth twitched. "Like maybe you think my
train's not on the right track."

"Is it?"

"Nope," he returned, without a trace of remorse.
"Now hurry up, Mags. Get changed. Time's
a-wasting."

"Can you just give me a clue as to what I should
wear?"

Cody's eyes lit with wicked amusement. "Your birthday suit?" he inquired hopefully, and Maggy flushed. "It was just a suggestion."

"Never mind," she returned, before heading toward her room. Maggy realized she had no idea how to dress, what to wear or where they were going! All she knew was that wherever they were going, she was going to be with Cody. And for now that seemed to be enough.

"Now Mags," Cody said as he refilled her wineglass. "You have to admit that this was a very logical idea."

Maggy laughed softly. "Cody, you are the only person in the world who would think having a picnic on the beach in the evening would be a logical idea."

"I'll have you know it's perfectly logical." Cody glanced around. "At night you don't have to worry about crowds or sunburn. Ants aren't really a problem, and it's not so darn hot. You can have just as much fun having a picnic under the moon as you can under the sun."

"I guess you're right," Maggy admitted, wondering why Cody was so interested in being logical all of a sudden. "Why couldn't you just tell me that at the house? Why the big mystery?"

Cody looked at her sheepishly. "Well, Mags, to tell you the truth, it wasn't really a mystery. But you were so down in the dumps when you came home, I thought a little teasing might cheer you up.''

"Oh Cody," she said softly, touched beyond measure. "You did cheer me up. You made me crazy for a few minutes there, but you cheered me up.''

"Good." He laughed and flashed her a wicked look. "Are you ready for your surprise now?''

"I'm not that cheerful," she retorted, looking at him suspiciously.

"Don't you notice anything?''

Blinking rapidly, Maggy stared up at him. Even in the descending darkness, she noticed a lot of things—the way his hair dipped boyishly over his forehead, the way his eyes glinted with desire or amusement, the way the man filled a room or a set of clothing. And she noticed the way his kisses and caresses set her heart pounding and her blood boiling, filling her with a longing that overshadowed everything but him.

"No," she admitted, not knowing what he was getting at.

"Look at me. Aren't I dressed sensibly?" His eyes twinkled with delight and Maggy blew out an exasperated sigh. She had a feeling the man was leading her down the primrose path—again.

"Yes," she admitted, laughing at the expectant look on his face. "You're dressed sensibly. And?" she prompted, not willing to admit that she had much preferred his state of dress that morning—or rather his state of undress.

"Well, Maggy, I thought I'd try it *your* way, for a change. We've got the whole weekend in front of us. I'm going to show you I can do things sensibly, logically and—" He glanced at her sheepishly.

"Rationally," Maggy supplied, touched that he found it necessary to try things her way in an effort to please her.

"Rationally," he repeated, as if trying to commit it to memory. "Now, for the logical thing, we're having a picnic—"

"Wait a minute." Maggy held up a hand to stop him. She had to attend to the matter at hand, before he dragged her any deeper into his shenanigans. And before she lost not only her sanity but her heart as well. "I appreciate your efforts, Cody, but I thought we were going to spend the weekend looking for a woman for you?"

"Honey," he said softly, pinning her with his gaze. "I think I've already *found* the woman for me." At his words her stomach dropped to her feet, and Maggy glanced away. His implication was so clear it made her heart soar, and at the same time increased her fear. There couldn't be anything between them, her mind raged. She couldn't afford to get involved with Cody—not now. They were two different people, with different ideas, different philosophies. Getting involved with Cody any further would not be logical, sensible or even rational, for that matter.

He was just like her mother, crazy, illogical and totally without regard for circumstances or consequences. To become involved with Cody any more than she already had would be courting disaster, not to mention indigestion!

Impulsively Maggy glanced up at him. Oh Lord, whom was she kidding! Her stomach contracted as realization hit her with the force of a blow. Like it or not, she was already involved with Cody, more than she could ever admit.

"Oh Cody," she breathed sadly, wishing things were different, but knowing they weren't. "I wish—"

"All right," he said hurriedly, not letting her finish. "I'll tell you what we'll do. We'll compromise. How does that sound?" He looked so full of the devil that Maggy felt another wave of suspicion. She had a feeling his idea of compromise might be her idea of disaster.

"I don't know," she said morosely. "I haven't heard enough of this compromise to decide."

He laughed softly. "Tonight will be ours, just yours and mine. Bobby's with your mom, and we're all alone. We're going to forget everything and just enjoy each other's company. I'll show you that I can be sensible, logical and—" he grinned "—rational, all right? Then tomorrow we can start looking for a woman. How does that sound?'' He was looking at her so expectantly that Maggy didn't have the heart to turn him down.

"I think that sounds wonderful," she admitted truthfully.

"Good." Leaning against a tree, Cody slid his arms around her and pulled her back against him. Maggy tensed for a moment, then relaxed as the heat of his body warmed hers. Stretching out her legs, Maggy leaned her head against his shoulder. They were silent for long moments, the only sound the rapid beating of their hearts in unison.

The moon was rising high over the crystal-blue lake. A few scattered stars began to twinkle against the backdrop of the darkening sky. Several boats dotting the horizon bobbed in the distance. The sound of the lake lapping slowly against the sand had a lulling effect on Maggy.

"You know," Cody said softly, "you never did tell me what you got caught reading."

Maggy sighed. This afternoon seemed so long ago, she had almost forgotten about the fiasco with Miss Barklay. "My boss—Miss Barklay—caught me reading one of your books."

She could feel him smiling in the darkness. "Which one?"

"*Wild Bill Cody's Amazing Adventures of the Amazon.*" Remembering the look on Miss Barklay's face, Maggy laughed. "If you could have seen her face, Cody, she was so appalled. *Adventures of the Amazon* wasn't exactly on the recommended reading list for Miss Avalon's Academy this semester.''

"No, I imagine not." Cody's voice quivered in amusement as he tightened his arms around her.

"Then, on top of everything else she found oat cereal in my hair. Remember when I was giving Bobby his breakfast?" Cody nodded, and Maggy went on. "Well, apparently a couple of pieces got stuck in my hair."

"And your boss found them?" Cody moved her around until she was lying in his arms, looking up at him.

"Oh, Cody." Maggy sighed heavily, meeting his gaze. "I did something so foolish." One dark brow rose in question and Maggy rushed on. "Miss Barklay confiscated your book, and I demanded she give it back to me."

"You didn't! Why Mags, I'm proud of you." She was warmed by his smile of approval.

"I can't believe I did that. I don't know, after today I just may have blown my chance to be headmistress." Maggy dropped her gaze, feeling an over-whelming sadness. "I've worked so hard for that position."

"Honey?" Cody lifted a hand and stroked her cheek. "You really like your job, don't you?" Maggy nodded as the palm of his hand gently caressed her cheek. She loved the feel of his rough hand against her smooth skin.

"Yes, I love it. But sometimes—" Maggy stopped, not wanting to put into words what she was feeling.

"Sometimes, what?" His eyes quietly searched her face.

"Sometimes," she began tentatively, "I just get tired of all the rules and restrictions that go with my position. Miss Barklay has such rigid requirements for her staff. Our actions have to be absolutely above reproach. Not just in our professional lives, but in our personal lives as well." It was the first time Maggy had ever openly admitted that part of her job filled her with displeasure. It felt good to talk to someone about it.

"Is that why you were so upset when your mother and I got arrested?"

Maggy nodded. "If my boss ever found out that it was my mother who was arrested in that fiasco, I'd probably be fired faster than a cabbie makes change."

Cody chuckled softly and gave her a quick hug. "Honey, you know there's a lot more to life than just rules and regulations. It seems to me that you've boxed yourself into a little corner, doing only what's expected of you." Cody cradled her face in his hand. "You know, life isn't just being sensible, rational and logical. Seems to me that you've got to learn how to have some fun, to enjoy life and take a chance on things. Honey," he said gently. "Life's a banquet and you're settling for crumbs."

His words hung in the air between them. For a long silent moment, Maggy simply stared into his eyes, listening to the water lap softly against the shore, feeling the soft breeze dance across her skin.

Was Cody right? she wondered. Had she boxed herself into a little corner, restricting herself only to the safe boundaries of her profession? Suddenly Maggy didn't know. Never before had she questioned her situation. Never before had she felt so restless or so unfulfilled.

She was confused and concerned, and suddenly terribly unsure of herself and her feelings.

"Oh, Cody," she whispered, reaching for him. His arms tightened around her, and she buried her face in his shoulder. What she wanted at this moment was to stop time forever, to stay right here in Cody's arms. In his arms she felt safe, free from rules and regulations, free from everything but the feelings tearing at her heart.

"Mags," Cody said softly, his large hand stroking her back. "I think you're too young to be so old. Having fun isn't against the law, neither is enjoying yourself. Seems to me you deserve a bit of both."

Did she? Maggy wondered, still clinging to Cody. Did she deserve to have some fun and enjoy herself?

Her job had always been so fulfilling that she'd never felt the need for anything else in her life. But now Maggy suddenly felt an ache, a loneliness that her job didn't seem to be able to fill.

"Mags, I've got responsibilities too, but that sure as hell doesn't mean I can't enjoy myself and have fun. You ought to learn how to do it, too." Cody was silent for a moment. "If you want," he said tentatively, causing Maggy to lift her head from his shoulder, "I could show you how to have fun—now don't look at me like that, Mags—I don't mean anything crazy, just nice, normal, everyday fun." Cody shrugged. "You're going to help me; I think it's only fair to return the favor."

"You'd do that?" Maggy asked, feeling touched despite the fact that she swore she wasn't going to get involved with him. He was only offering to teach her to have fun, she reminded herself, trying to stop the wave of uncertainty that bubbled inside. He wasn't asking for a lifelong commitment. How could it hurt?

"Sure." He grinned. "I'll tell you what. Tomorrow I thought we'd drive into Chicago and hit some theatrical agencies. Your mom still has some contacts in the industry and we might be able to find a woman. Afterward, we'll have some fun. What do you say?"

The idea of finding a woman for Cody was slowly losing all appeal, but Maggy nodded, suddenly feeling very lighthearted. She was going to help Cody, and in his own way he was going to help her.

"It's a deal then." Cody leaned forward and planted a soft kiss on her lips. "We'd better get back," he said, his eyes searching hers as if he wanted to say more, but didn't. "Elizabeth should be getting home with Bobby pretty soon." Cody stood up and began to gather their things. Maggy bent over to fold the picnic blanket.

"Tell me, Mags, have you ever had a Fuzzy Navel?"

She jerked upright. "I beg your pardon?"

"A Fuzzy Navel," Cody repeated, looking at her curiously.

"What does fuzz in my navel have to do with anything?" she cried in alarm. "You promised nothing crazy!" she accused, and Cody threw back his head and laughed.

"No, no, no. It's got nothing to do with *your* navel, or anybody else's." He leaned forward and spoke directly into her alarmed face. "It's a drink, Mags. Just a drink. And a pretty good one at that."

"A drink, huh?" she repeated, looking at him skeptically, and wondering just what kind of a drink would have such a ridiculous name.

"Scout's honor." Cody lifted his hand in the air as if he were taking an oath. "Would this face lie?" he inquired, trying hard to contain his grin.

"Yes," Maggy said honestly, and Cody chuckled,

looping an arm around her neck again as they started up the beach.

"Wait until I tell you about the Tennessee Twins," he whispered, and Maggy smiled. She was on to him now.

"Another drink?" she replied confidently.

"No," Cody said with a grin. "It's two sisters back home, and Mags, you should see the set of—"

"Cody!" Maggy cried, giving him a poke with her elbow. Good Lord! Now what had she let this wild man talk her into?

Chapter Seven

"**W**hat about her?" Cody asked with a frown, studying the black-and-white picture in his hand. They had spent most of the morning going from one theatrical agency to another, looking for the right woman for him. Maggy peered at the picture over his shoulder and shook her head. "I don't think so," she said, surveying the picture carefully. "Her coloring is all wrong. Besides," she added. "She looks much too cool and sophisticated to be a mother." There, that sounded like a logical explanation, Maggy reasoned. The glance Cody flashed her told her otherwise.

"Maggy." Smiling, Cody sighed her name. "We have been to every theatrical agency in the city of Chicago. This is our last hope. You've found fault with every single actress available. Now, we don't have much time—less than three weeks,'' he remind her. ''We're going to have to settle on someone.''

Cody was right. They were going to have to settle on someone. But not *this* someone, Maggy decided, studying the picture again. She had to admit Cody was right. She *had* found fault with every single woman that had been available. Maggy couldn't help it. The thought of another woman being involved with Cody and Bobby was enough to bring on a fit of acute jealousy that she couldn't explain or deny.

All Maggy knew was that she felt protective and possessive about the two men who had suddenly catapulted themselves into her life. And despite her ridiculous behavior, she didn't want to share Cody and Bobby with another woman for *any* reason.

''Mags, look.'' Cody poked her with his elbow, and she glanced up. A petite blonde with a knockout figure had entered the office and was now standing at the receptionist's desk, talking to the secretary. The woman's pose was practiced and polished, designed to show off her best features. ''What about her?'' Cody whispered.

Maggy's eyes widened in disbelief. This woman was hardly mother material, she thought, taking in the tight black miniskirt and matching tunic top. She looked more like centerfold material, Maggy acknowledged sourly, feeling her heart constrict.

"Mags?" Cody was watching the blonde, and Maggy was watching Cody. "She's about the right age, and her coloring is right. What do you think?"

What she was thinking at the moment would probably turn Cody's ears blue. Maggy chewed her bottom lip. She knew she had to come up with a good reason to convince Cody this woman wasn't right.

"Cody," she stammered, narrowing her eyes as she studied the woman. "I don't think she's quite right."

"How will we know if we don't talk to her? Come on." Grabbing her hand, Cody pulled her toward the other woman. "Excuse me," he said politely, and the woman turned to face them. She took one look at Cody and a coquettish smile lifted her lips.

"Well, hello there," she purred softly. Her voice was low and breathy. Maggy rolled her eyes.

"Ma'am," Cody said politely. "I'm looking for an actress—"

"Well, sugar, *I'm* an actress." The woman flicked a dismissive glance at Maggy, then turned her attention back to Cody. "My name's Priscilla. And I'm...available." Her gaze ran the length of Cody, and she smiled in approval. "What did you have in mind?" Leaning close, she draped one perfectly manicured hand possessively on Cody's bare arm. Maggy pursed her lips in annoyance. Obviously Prissy Priscilla was more interested in Cody than in the job he had to offer. Maggy felt a wave of anger.

The woman was flashy and obvious, and she was clinging to Cody like lint to a bad suit! If Maggy didn't do something—and fast—the woman would be... Oh Lord, what was she going to do?

"Would you excuse us?" Maggy asked. After forcing a bright smile, Maggy slowly peeled Priscilla's hand from Cody's arm, then dragged Cody into a corner. "Cody, you can't possibly be seriously considering...Priscilla," she hissed. She deliberately spoke the name as if the woman were something that belonged in a specimen bottle.

"Why not, honey?" he inquired. "She's about the right age, seems to be pleasant enough, and she sure looks like she'd photograph well." He was craning his neck to look at Priscilla and Maggy jerked his arm to regain his attention.

"No," Maggy insisted, glancing up to find Priscilla watching them intently. "Sh-she's just not right." The woman smiled and wiggled her fingers at Cody. Maggy steered him around so his back was to Priscilla. Somehow she had to dissuade Cody. The woman was too pert, too pretty and just entirely too cute for words. Maggy felt an instant dislike for her.

"We can't be too picky, Mags," Cody said.

"You know we don't have much time left. She really seems perfect. Don't you think so?"

Perfect? Maggy glanced up at her and felt her spirits nosedive. That was the problem, she realized dismally. Prissy Priscilla *was* perfect.

"Her nose is all wrong," Maggy grumbled, grasping at straws in an effort to discourage him.

"Her nose, you say?" Cody repeated, with a lift of his brow. He was working hard to keep the amusement out of his eyes and the grin off his face. "You're not jealous are you, Mags?" he asked, bending down to whisper with an ear-to-ear grin on his face.

"I'm not jealous," she insisted heatedly, knowing it was a lie. She was so jealous, she wouldn't be surprised if her skin turned green. "It's just… just…that she just doesn't seem the type. Look at her figure," she whispered, turning around to look at Priscilla. Cody's eyes followed hers. "On second thought," Maggy grumbled, turning him around again, "maybe you'd better not." She tried another tactic. "Cody, do you really expect someone to believe that body has had a baby?"

Deep down, Maggy knew she was being totally irrational and unfair, not to mention illogical, but she couldn't help it. Her mind got the message, but the message clearly wasn't getting to her vulnerable heart.

"Well, the least we can do is talk to her. What

could it hurt?'' Cody asked, grabbing her hand and dragging her back to Priscilla. It was do or die, Maggy realized glumly. She was not about to turn Cody and Bobby over to this woman. She'd sooner trust a rabbit in a garden of lettuce than this female with Cody and Bobby!

''Tell me, Priscilla,'' Maggy said, deciding to jump in with both feet before Cody could open his mouth. ''How do you feel about children?''

''Children?'' Priscilla whispered, paling visibly.

''Yes, children,'' Maggy repeated with relish. ''You know, those messy little people who need to be fed and changed, burped and bathed.''

''Mags!'' Cody growled, but she ignored him. She could almost feel the wind from Prissy Priscilla's retreating feet, and she wasn't about to stop now.

''We're speaking of one child in particular,'' Maggy explained helpfully. ''He's two years old and cute as a button. Of course, you do realize that children at this age behave more like puppies than people. They wet and bite, but that shouldn't be a problem, should it?'' Maggy asked sweetly.

''I...I...mmm...allergic to children,'' Priscilla mumbled, inching away from them as if they had something contagious. ''My agent knows—it's clearly specified in my contract that I don't have to work with...'' Priscilla swallowed convulsively.

"Children," she whispered. "They're messy and noisy, and…" Her voice trailed off.

Maggy turned to Cody, giving him a look that said *I told you so*. "See what I mean?" she whispered, watching as Priscilla continued her hasty retreat.

Crossing his arms over his chest, Cody grinned down at her, and shook his head. "Well, Mags, I've got to hand it to you. That was some performance."

"Performance?" Maggy repeated blankly. "I really don't know what you're talking about," she said airily, taking Cody firmly by the arm and hustling him toward the door. "She really didn't look like the motherly type, Cody."

"No, I guess not," he admitted, grinning at her wickedly. "I'm sure your vast store of information on Bobby's behavior had nothing to do with her hesitancy, either."

"Of course not," Maggy confirmed, deciding to jump to a more neutral subject. "Cody," she said with a sigh, "I'm really tired, and we *have* had a full day. Why don't we go back home?" she suggested. "It's still early and it's such a beautiful day. Why don't we get Bobby and spend the afternoon by the pool?" Maggy knew she was babbling, but she didn't care. She wanted Cody out and away from Prissy Priscilla before he had a chance to change his mind. "We can have a barbecue, go for a swim and just relax. Maybe even have some fun. What do you say?'' Without giving him a chance to answer, Maggy yanked open the door and dragged Cody through it, feeling an inexplicable sense of relief.

"More dogs?'' Bobby asked, grabbing at Maggy's legs as he shoved the last of his hot dog into his mouth.

"No more dogs, tiger,'' Cody growled, tucking his hands behind his head as he sprawled lazily in the hammock. "You've already had two,'' Cody admonished without opening his eyes.

"Damn.'' Bobby's lips turned down and Maggy immediately reached for him.

"Come here, Sport.'' Settling the baby comfortably on her lap Maggy checked to be sure Cody's eyes were still closed before reaching for another hot dog off the patio table.

"More dogs, Ma-ma?'' Bobby asked hopefully, looking up at her with big, pleading eyes. Chuckling softly, Maggy held a finger to her lips to quiet him.

"Shh,'' she cautioned. Grinning from ear to ear, Bobby took the little bites of hot dog she handed him and happily stuffed them into his mouth.

Smiling at the bliss on the toddler's face, Maggy inhaled deeply, savoring the scent of the late-summer blooms that filled the grounds of her mother's estate. After the fiasco at the theatrical agency, they had returned to Lake Geneva, rescued

Bobby from his nap and spent the afternoon together just swimming and enjoying themselves.

Relaxed and comfortable, Maggy felt totally at peace with herself. Being with Cody and Bobby seemed to bring a lightness to her heart. Oh, how she enjoyed being with them! She felt so free when Cody and Bobby were around. Free from rules and regulations, free from all responsibilities. It was a freedom she hadn't known was possible in her hitherto restricted life.

"You're going to spoil that boy," Cody drawled, and Maggy jumped guiltily. Opening one eye, Cody grinned at her.

"How did you know?" she asked with a laugh, giving Bobby the last of his contraband hot dog. Unconsciously she stroked the baby's head.

"Intuition." His eyes met hers. "You know, Mags," he said, lifting his head to get a better look at her. "You're really good with him."

"Thank you," she said with a smile. "So are you."

"Honey." He laughed, leaning on one elbow and crossing one bare foot over the other. "I've had lots of practice. Bobby's been with me since he was a year old, but even before that he spent more time with me than he did with his mother." Cody was silent for a moment. "Pearl's not a bad woman, just a bit mixed up. She was too young to take care of a baby.''

''So you assumed responsibility for him.'' Maggy glanced up at him, feeling her admiration and respect for him grow. His eyes caught and held hers for a long, silent moment, and her heart beat a wild rhythm in her chest. She could hear her own breath coming short and heavy in the still air.

Her two-piece bathing suit offered little covering. She could feel the way his look touched her, sliding down her slender frame and warming her almost as if Cody's hands were traveling over her instead of his gaze. Her blood seemed to heat up as it coursed quickly through her veins. In an effort to do something to distract herself, Maggy wrapped her arms tighter around Bobby and rocked him on her knees as a hot shiver skittered over her delicate skin.

''Mags,'' Cody said softly. ''If you're so good with kids, why is it you don't have any of your own?''

Maggy glanced up at him sharply. Suddenly she realized how much she missed having a family of her own; a man of her own. She had her job at the academy, her mother and her various charitable activities. She had thought her life was complete. Now she was vividly aware that something *had* been missing in her life...love.

Startled at her train of thought, Maggy shrugged,

trying to remain nonchalant. "I guess I've just been
too busy with my career."

"Can't you have a career and a family of your
own?"

"I never really thought about it," she conceded,
shifting uncomfortably. Maggy didn't want to admit
that before Cody and Bobby had roared into her life,
she had never considered having both. "How about
you?" she inquired. "Why aren't you married?"

"I don't know," Cody said with a heavy sigh.
"There's not many women willing to take on me
and a baby." He grinned at the thought and Maggy
found herself smiling, knowing how she had reacted
when she had first met Cody—how intimidated and
off balance she had been. Cody *did* have that effect,
she realized with amusement. Cody was outrageous,
reckless and totally charming, not to mention irresistible. "I guess a woman would have to be pretty
special to accept and love both of us. Bobby and I
come as a package." He raised his brows. "You
know, baby makes three."

How could someone not accept and love both of
them? Maggy asked herself, glancing down with affection at Bobby who was snuggled up in her lap,
almost asleep. Smoothing back his hair, Maggy bent
and kissed his head. The child had quickly earned a
permanent place in her heart, and Maggy knew without a doubt that any woman would be lucky to have
Cody and Bobby in her life, to have their love. She

pushed the thought back to the far corners of her
mind. Yes, any woman would be lucky, she thought
wistfully, knowing *she* could never be that woman.
She had agreed to help him, and she had agreed to
let him help her, but Maggy knew she had to keep
out of Cody's arms, and keep him out of her heart.

Her mind knew all the logical reasons, all the rational reasons; they were too different, their philosophies of life too far apart. While she led her life
based on rules and regulations, Cody on the other
hand deliberately ran his without any rules or regulations. When he wasn't within eyesight, Maggy
knew and accepted all the logical reasons she
shouldn't get involved with him. But, Lord, when
he was here, grinning down at her, doing his best to
charm her into agreeing with him, Maggy felt her
resistance blow away like a kite on a windy day.

"Bobby and I, we do all right," Cody went on.
"Except when I get myself in a fix like the one I'm
in now with *Modern Motherhood*." Maggy could
hear the humor in his voice and wondered again if
perhaps she had been just a bit rash in her refusal
to accept the award for him. The thought had been
playing around the corners of her mind all day, ever
since they had left the theatrical agency and Prissy
Priscilla.

"Cody?" she asked suddenly as a thought occurred to her. "Do the editors of *Modern Motherhood* know you're a man?"

"Well, yes." He grinned. "And no. That's another whole set of problems and another whole long story. You're probably not going to think this story is too logical or sensible, either."

"Probably not," she agreed with a smile. "But go ahead and tell me anyway."

"See, I write under the name of Bea Cody for *Modern Motherhood*, and—"

"What's the *B* for?" Maggy asked with a frown, knowing Cody's penchant for telling stories in bits and pieces. She didn't want this story to get away from her.

"No, not *B* the letter, Bea as in Beatrice. It was my mother's name," he went on to explain. "And since most of the advice I learned about mothering came from her, I thought it only fair to give her some of the credit. I guess the editors just assumed I was a woman, and I haven't exactly told them any different. What my sex was didn't seem important. I consider myself Bobby's mother and father. See, the magazine relies heavily on the publicity generated every year from the contest. It not only helps their circulation but boosts their advertising revenues, too. The winner gets her picture taken with the editors accepting the award and the scholarship. That's one of the reasons that award has to be accepted in person. So you can see why I've got to find a woman." Cody quietly swayed back and forth for a moment, staring off into space. "That award means a lot to me, Mags, not only because of the scholarship but because mothers are real special people to me. I wouldn't want to do anything to embarrass the editors or anyone from the magazine.''

Maggy nodded, understanding a little better why Cody was so desperate to find a woman. She looked up at him and found him watching her. The more she learned about the man, the more she was learning to care about him. And, she realized, there was nothing she could do to stop her feelings.

''Why did you agree to help me, Mags?'' he asked finally, bringing his eyes back to hers.

Why indeed? she wondered. Was it only to keep an eye on her mother and keep her out of trouble, as she'd claimed? Or did her reasons go deeper than that? Maggy knew the answer, but she wasn't sure she was ready or willing to admit such a thing. Not to herself, or to Cody.

''For my mother's sake.'' She was never very good at lying, and feared he could see right through her words. ''Cody, I understand why you want to do this,'' she said quickly, anxious to change the subject. ''I really do. I can see how important Bobby and his future are to you. In fact, I kind of admire what you're doing,'' she said softly, causing Cody to sit up abruptly. He threw his long legs over the side of the hammock and looked at her curiously.

"You do?" His voice was so surprised that she laughed.

"I do."

He cocked his head, his eyes twinkling in delight. "Even though it's not sensible or reasonable?"

"Yes, even though it's not sensible or reasonable," Maggy admitted, finally realizing that being sensible and reasonable had its place, but not necessarily in Cody's life. What he was doing was so right, so wonderful, it really didn't matter whether it was sensible or reasonable.

"Well I'll be..." Cody muttered, looking at her in surprise. The look on his face took her breath away, and Maggy directed her attention to Bobby who was fast asleep in her arms. "Is your mother the only reason you agreed to help me?" he asked, and Maggy had a feeling he was asking a whole lot more than just one question.

"No," she said carefully. "I...I don't want to see Bobby lose that scholarship."

"Are those the only reasons?" he asked hopefully, and Maggy could see a mischievous smile on his lips. Cody was direct if nothing else, she thought humorously, smoothing back Bobby's hair. She knew what he was asking. Cody wanted to know if the reasons for her help extended to him and her feelings for him. She tried to remind her heart of all the reasons she couldn't get involved with him, but her heart didn't appear to be paying much attention.

Aware that he was watching her carefully, Maggy glanced away, deciding the best course of action was to change gears. Quickly. "Cody, what are you and Bobby going to do after the award ceremony?"

"Do?" he asked with a frown, clearly not understanding.

"Are you going to go back to Tennessee?"

Cody looked at her intently, his eyes warm and serious. "That depends."

"On what?"

"A lot of things." Cody swayed gently in the hammock, letting his eyes slide over her until a slumbering wave of heat shimmied over her skin. "I don't like to make plans too far in advance," he told her. "I kind of like to take each day as it comes."

Well, Maggy mused, so much for being nosy. She had no more of an idea what Cody was going to do now then she had before.

"How do you manage to write and still take care of Bobby?" she asked, deciding to be nosy for just a little while longer, or until she got some answers— whichever came first. "Do you have help?"

Cody threw back his head and laughed. "Help? Honey, do you think that little tiger would be as attached to me, or you for that matter, if someone else was taking care of him?" Cody shook his head. "After Pearl ran off, Bobby went through a bad period. He'd stand by the window and cry for his mama for hours. It tore my heart out," Cody said quietly, and Maggy instinctively tightened her arms around Bobby, feeling an unexpected pain for him. "From the day Pearl left it's just been me and him. I spend almost every waking moment with him. During the day we go to the park or the pool, or just play in the yard. At night, when he's asleep, I write."

"Oh, Cody," she breathed softly, realizing just how special the man was.

"Bobby's out like a light," he said quietly. "I think we'd better put him to bed." She started to rise, but Cody slid off the hammock and crossed over to her lounge chair.

"I'll do it, Mags. You've done so much for him. You stay put. Sit and relax for a few moments. It's so beautiful out; maybe we can have some…fun?" One brow rose wickedly as he scooped Bobby out of her arms and headed toward the house.

Cody and Bobby had inserted themselves in her life so quickly, Maggy thought with a smile, watching Cody. It was no longer just herself and her mother but the four of them.

What was she going to do? Maggy wondered dismally, absently picking up a blade of grass. She still had to find a woman for Cody; her mind knew it, but her heart didn't want another woman involved with Cody or Bobby, for any reason. Emotionally, Maggy knew she was headed for heartbreak. She was more attached to Bobby than she had a right to be. And to Cody, her mind echoed.

If Cody went back to Tennessee… When Cody went back to Tennessee… Her mind pushed back the unpleasant thought.

Being with Cody had enabled her to see for the first time that life didn't have to be lived only according to someone else's rules and regulations. Not every action had to be sensible, logical and rational. What Cody wanted to do in order to insure Bobby's future wasn't any of those things, but Maggy knew in her heart it was right—oh, so right.

For the first time in her life, Maggy wished she could be more like her mother. She wished she could let her heart rule her head. But old habits die hard, and Maggy knew she wasn't quite ready yet to toss aside all that she had worked for in order to do what her heart wanted.

"Mags?" Cody's voice brought her back to the present. "Ready for some fun?" Cody's long legs carried him in quick strides to her side. She fixed her eyes on the dark hair on his broad chest that narrowed down and disappeared into the tiny scrap of black material he insisted was a bathing suit. Trying to gather her scattered thoughts, Maggy smiled up at him and took the hand he offered.

Without warning, Cody gave a whoop and then picked her up in his arms.

"Put me down!" she cried, clasping her arms

around his neck as he walked toward the pool. With a wicked smile in his eyes, Cody sauntered down the steps at a leisurely pace until he stood waist deep in water. "Don't you dare drop me!" Maggy warned, trying to look stern but failing miserably.

Grinning lecherously into her startled face, Cody bent and dipped her into the water so that her entire back, legs and neck were wet. She let out another screech as the cool water lapped against her warm skin.

"Mags," Cody said with amusement. "Didn't your mother ever tell you screeching wasn't logical, rational or even sensible?"

"Neither is drowning a person," she returned, giving his bare chest a thump. Laughing, Cody walked deeper into the water, and she tightened her arms around him.

"Mags, this is the fun part."

"No, it's not," she insisted, shivering. "We can't go into the pool," she protested, trying to struggle out of his arms. He held on tight. "Bobby might need us."

Cody laughed. "Nice try, Mags. But your mother's in the house with him. She's sitting right in the living room doing a crossword puzzle."

Maggy looked at him skeptically. "My mother doing a crossword puzzle?" She shook her head. "Must have the wrong mother. Mine's never done anything so tame in her life."

"People change, you know," he said softly, and Maggy had a feeling he was not talking just about her mother.

"Are you sure?" she inquired, trying to divert his attention from whatever devious plan he had cooked up for her.

"I'm positive," he assured her, holding her tighter and ignoring her struggling as he moved still deeper into the water. "She just asked me for a five-letter word for responsible."

She frowned. "A five-letter word for responsible?" Maggy repeated, still confused by her mother's seemingly peaceful activity.

"A five-letter word for responsible is..." He paused and grinned into her face, clearly enjoying himself. "*Maggy.*"

"Maggy?" she echoed dully. It took a moment for his meaning to sink in. "I am not a five-letter word for responsible!" she insisted, thumping his chest again.

"Yes, you are," he assured her, twirling her around in the water, and getting her wetter and wetter. "You're responsible, reliable, sensible and all those other good things. Why, you're solid as a rock and just as dependable. A person could set his watch by you, Mags."

"You make me sound like a damned insurance company," Maggy grumbled, and he threw back his head and laughed. Was that how Cody saw her? she wondered. She wasn't an insurance company, Maggy thought defiantly. She was a healthy, normal young woman! And maybe it was about time Cody realized it. She looked into his eyes and saw the tenderness there. She decided it would be prudent not to argue the point with him. If he thought of her that way, it was her own fault and up to her to change his mind.

"Now Mags, do you really think I'd drown you?" he asked, looking too mischievous for her peace of mind.

"Yes!" she cried, hanging on to him tighter. She could feel the prickly hairs on his chest tickle the skin bared by her swimsuit.

Cody came to an abrupt halt and lowered her to her feet. Her breath caught as she slid down his long, muscular length. Slipping his arms around her waist, Cody pulled her close until her bare toes touched his. It sent a shiver through her.

"*Drowning,*" he whispered, letting his eyes capture hers, "wasn't quite what I had in mind to do with you, Mags."

His words were so soft, so sincere that for a moment Maggy couldn't speak. She held his gaze, despite the fact that her knees had grown weak and her heart pumped at a frantic pace. A faint breeze whispered through the yard; the scent of blooming flowers rolled over them. Everything was still, quiet, except for the quiet sound of their breathing. Her breasts rose and fell with her labored breathing.

Cody reached for her, holding her small hand gently in his, caressing her palm with one callused thumb. Tremors raced up her arm, and Maggy inhaled sharply.

She touched his cheek as a deep, aching warmth seeped into her heart. "Cody." His name came out on a breathy whisper. His eyes widened, darkened as she whispered his name again. Standing on tiptoe, and ignoring the cool pool water lapping against her, Maggy moved her hands to his bare chest, leaned forward and lifted her lips to his. So much for resolutions, she thought hazily, sliding her arms around him.

With a groan, Cody hauled her body closer to his until her feet were dangling off the ground. His mouth covered hers so urgently that she didn't know where her breath stopped and his began.

She leaned into him, her softness straining against his hardness, savoring and enjoying every inch, every feeling that rolled over her. She responded to his kisses, allowing his mouth to possess and claim her. His tongue, ever gentle, drew sensuous circles against one corner of her mouth until her lips parted in welcome. Her breath shuddered out of her parted lips, and she swayed against him, threading her fingers through the silky strands of his hair. Cody's hands slid upward, until they framed her face. His fingers stroked her cheeks, touching her as if he couldn't believe she was real.

"Mags," he whispered, pulling his lips from hers. Wide-eyed, she looked up at him, lost in his eyes, lost in the feelings for him that were overwhelming her.

Cody leaned his forehead against hers, his breathing sharp and ragged. He sighed deeply and tried to laugh. It came out somewhere between a groan and a growl. "What would Miss Barklay say?" he asked, trying to make light of the situation.

"I don't give two figs for what she'd say," Maggy returned, giving Cody a slow smile and reaching for him again. As his lips found hers, Maggy groaned softly, realizing that she really didn't care what Miss Barklay would say. What she was doing now wasn't sensible, logical or rational. But Maggy didn't care.

At the moment the only thing she cared about was the man in her arms.

All too soon, Cody lifted his lips from hers and Maggy blinked up at him. "Is this the fun part?" she asked hazily, and Cody grinned. A grin she would have recognized if her mind hadn't been so foggy.

"No," he said slowly, advancing even closer to her. "This is." Cody grabbed her around the waist, and with a whoop of delight dunked her mightily in the pool.

Chapter Eight

Restlessly Maggy rolled over in bed, tucked her arms under her head and stared at the ceiling. It had been nearly three and a half weeks since Cody had burst into her life, and they still hadn't found a woman for him.

They'd made efforts to look, but somehow Maggy had always managed to find fault with each candidate. This one was too tall, that one too short. Another had shifty eyes, and yet another had the wrong coloring. There were only two days left, and they were no closer to finding a woman now than they had been at the beginning.

Guilt engulfed Maggy, and she sighed heavily. She had to admit that any one of the women they had found would do, but the idea of another woman, *any* woman being involved with Cody and Bobby was enough to make her break out in hives.

Maggy knew she had changed in the past few weeks. While she still took pleasure in her work, it was the time spent with Cody and Bobby that had become meaningful.

Her days at the academy seemed to inch along at a snail's pace. Her life now seemed to revolve around Cody and Bobby. This wasn't the first time she found it an effort to recall what her life had been like before Cody and Bobby.

Dull, she decided. Her life had been dull and boring. Maggy had come to realize that she had been sleepwalking through life, worrying so much about rules and regulations and silly things like being sensible and rational that she'd never taken the time to enjoy herself. As Cody had told her on their first picnic, *life was a banquet, and she had been settling for crumbs.*

For the first time in her life Maggy was enjoying herself, and her life. And she knew Cody was the reason.

And Bobby. Maggy adjusted her pillow and smiled. She was hopelessly in love with the little urchin, and apparently the feeling was mutual. Bobby was so attached to her that leaving for work every day had become an upheaval. Bobby cried for her, and Maggy felt herself racked with guilt, torn between wanting to stay home with him, which she really wanted to do, and going off to work, which she knew she had to do. Now she knew how other mothers felt.

Other mothers.

The words echoed in her mind. She loved Bobby so much, in some ways she felt like his mother. While there were no blood ties between them the feelings she had for the child couldn't be any stronger if she *were* his mother.

Love. The word had been drifting in and out of her thoughts for days, weeks. Maggy knew in her heart that Bobby wasn't the only one she had fallen in love with.

Maggy lay in the darkness, her heart pounding in sudden fear. She was in love with Cody. She turned over again, her eyes wide open and afraid.

How had it happened? When did it happen?

Her mind went over all the good times they had shared during the past few weeks. Cody had kept her so busy, she'd barely had time to worry about her mother, or about rules and regulations for that matter.

They had gone on night picnics, fished in the quiet early hours just before dawn—despite the fact that Maggy flinched at the sight of a worm and nearly swooned when she caught a fish. They had even built a bonfire on the beach and roasted marsh-mallows, even though the weather alone was hot enough to roast a body, let alone a marshmallow.

She had roller-skated into town in broad daylight, with Bobby strapped on her back and Cody's hand clenched tightly in hers. Cody had even talked her into drinking a Fuzzy Navel. And despite its name, it had been good. Even though it made her lips feel as if they were going to slide off her face.

Cody hadn't changed; the man was reckless and outrageous, and he could still drown her in his charm with just a smile, just a touch. But he was also warm and gentle, one of the kindest men she'd ever met. No, Cody hadn't changed. She had.

She was in love with Cody. The thought was so clear, so vivid Maggy didn't know why she hadn't realized it before.

Oh Lord, Maggy thought as her heart filled with sadness. Even though she was in love with Cody, that didn't change who *she* was, and who *he* was.

Cody hadn't said so in so many words, but Maggy couldn't help but wonder what would happen when they did find a woman for him. Would he go back to Tennessee? The thought left her feeling sad and desolate. In just a few days Cody could be gone from her life as quickly as he'd entered it, and all she would have were her memories of him. She was running out of time.

She'd still have her job, Maggy reminded herself, and her position at the academy, but she knew that it wouldn't be enough. Not anymore.

A sudden crack of thunder shook the silent house

and Maggy expelled a sigh of relief. Despite the air conditioning the house was hot and oppressive, and a good storm would surely help cool things off.

"Ma-ma." A soft whimpering filtered through the house and Maggy bolted upright in bed. Bobby. Her heart lurched and she was out of bed instantly, hurrying down the long hallway to the guest room that Cody and Bobby shared. Tiptoeing softly so as not to wake Cody, Maggy crossed the room, not daring to look at Cody who lay sprawled on his back across the bed. The covers were in a heap on the floor, and one arm was carelessly thrown over his face. His breathing was deep and steady, and Maggy quickly glanced away, directing her attention to the other male in the room, who apparently needed her attention.

"Ma-ma," Bobby whimpered. His eyes were red and his lower lip quivered. Big, glistening tears slid down his flushed cheeks, dripping off the end of his trembling chin. "Ma-ma," he said again, crawling quickly across the portable crib she had bought for him and pulling himself upright to reach for her.

"Shh Sport, don't cry," Maggy crooned, picking him up and planting a soft kiss on his damp cheek. "Did the thunder scare you?" she asked in a whisper, tiptoeing out of the room and down the stairs. "It's just a storm, Sport," she assured him as he wrapped his arms around her neck and clung to her. "It's nothing to worry about. Don't be scared."

Maggy buried her face in his hair, savoring his baby scent and knowing her heart was full to the brim with love for this child.

Cradling him in her arms, she pushed open the kitchen door. Quietly Maggy began to pace the room with him, murmuring soothing words and holding him tight. Bobby's eyelids drooped in spite of his best efforts to keep them open. Smiling in the darkness, Maggy stroked his head and continued pacing.

"Sweet baby," she murmured, dropping a kiss on his damp face. "Don't worry," she crooned in a soft voice. "Mama's here." The words echoed in the dark, quiet room and, blinking back tears, Maggy took a long, loving look at the child in her arms.

Pressing another kiss to his damp cheek, Maggy's eyes closed and she let her lips linger on his sweet-smelling skin. She would never forget his baby scent. Maggy tried to brand this moment permanently into her mind. She wanted to remember forever this time with her child.

Her child.

Oh, Lord, how she loved this child, she thought, hugging him tighter. Her throat ached with sudden tears.

But she *was* going to lose him, Maggy realized, feeling the pain as deeply and acutely as if the child were born of her own flesh and blood. Tears brimmed in her eyes, then spilled down her cheek.

She would change the way things were, but she

knew it was beyond her. As soon as she found a woman for Cody—and she had less than three days left to do it—oh Lord, Maggy thought sadly, pacing the floor frantically. What was she going to do?

Cody was who he was, and she was who she was, each caught up in their own circumstances; she with her job and her rules and regulations, he with his own life where rules and regulations had no place.

Her heart ached with a sadness that seeped into her very soul. It was so unfair. She had only just found love, and she was going to lose it. Tears welled again in her eyes and a sob caught in her throat.

"What's wrong with Bobby?" Cody demanded, pushing open the kitchen door. Startled, Maggy whirled around and stared at him. Cody's feet were as bare as his chest, and he had obviously just dragged on his jeans; the top snap was open, and the zipper not fully zipped. His black hair was mussed, his eyes were sleepy and tired, making him look—despite his size—all too vulnerable and appealing. The sight of him never failed to raise her pulse rate.

Cody looked so alarmed that she gave him a watery smile. "Shh," she ordered, pressing a finger to her lips to silence him and brushing away her tears before he saw them. "Bobby's fine. The storm just scared him."

Cody looked at her blankly, rubbing one eye.

"What storm?" he asked, shifting his weight sleepily from one foot to the other. She loved him so!

"Go back to bed, Cody," she instructed shakily, trying to shoo him out of the room before he saw her tears. "I'll take care of Bobby. He's almost asleep, and once I'm sure he's out I'll just put him back to bed."

"Mags?" Cody said cautiously, coming closer to inspect her face in the darkness. "What's wrong? Are you crying?" He lifted a hand and touched her cheek.

"No," she lied, glancing away. She didn't want him to see her pain.

"Honey, what's wrong?" Cody pulled out a chair, scraping it against the oak floor and ignoring her alarmed look as he tugged at her hand and pulled her—Bobby and all—into his lap. "Now I know why Bobby was crying," he whispered in the darkness, slipping his arms around her waist to stop her from getting free. "But I don't know why you're crying. And don't tell me you're not," he growled, when she opened her mouth to protest. "Hot as it is, that sure isn't sweat dripping from your lashes." His eyes, dark with concern and soft with tenderness, caressed her face, going over every inch until her senses were aflame.

Cody's scent, distinctively masculine, engulfed her. Savoring the scent, Maggy held it to her like a precious secret.

How long? she wondered, glancing away. How long until…?

Cody shifted his weight, and her breasts, covered only by the thin cotton of her nightgown, were pressed against his masculine chest. She could feel the beating of his heart against hers. Cody lifted one hand and gently wiped a tear from her cheek. It was her undoing.

"Oh, Cody," she whispered, dropping her head to his bare shoulder. A flash of lightning lit the room for a moment, and Maggy slid one arm around Cody, holding on to the sleeping Bobby for dear life as her tears came, dripping down her cheeks and staining Cody's bare skin. She knew she couldn't tell him why she was crying. She had gotten so used to sharing everything with Cody, talking everything over with him, that not being able to share this— her new feeling—seemed strange. Odd—she suddenly felt very alone.

The rain started, pelting the house in torrents. The wind howled through the trees as if echoing Maggy's pain. The rain continued and so did her tears. But Cody said nothing, holding her until her sobs quieted. Sniffling hard, she lifted her pounding head and tried to dry his wet shoulder.

"I'm sorry," she said weakly, trying to give him a smile. She was supposed to have helped him, but all she had done was fall in love with him. Some help she was.

"So am I, Mags. Sorry because I don't have the faintest idea what's got you so upset. Did I do something to hurt you, honey?" he asked, his voice genuinely concerned. Maggy gave him a weak smile. He hadn't done anything to hurt her yet. But she knew that soon enough, without meaning to, he would.

"No, Cody, you didn't do anything." It wasn't really a lie, she reasoned. He *hadn't* done anything. And couldn't do anything about the way she felt about him and Bobby. Nor could he do anything about the fact that no matter what happened she was going to be left alone, and lonely, with a very broken heart.

"Honey," he said cautiously, tipping her head up to look at her. "You were crying like your heart was about to break. Please, Mags, tell me what's got you so upset? You're not worried about your mother, are you?"

"No," she said softly, looking into his eyes. She wished her worries were that simple. Her eyes brimmed with tears again, despite her efforts to stop them.

"We're running out of time," she blubbered, laying her head on his shoulder again.

"Running out of time?" he repeated, frowning in confusion. "Time for what?" he asked, clearly not understanding, but trying desperately.

"To find you a woman." And, she added mentally, time was running out for them. He would be gone soon, with Bobby and...

"Is that what's got you so upset?" he asked incredulously, drawing back to look at her. Feeling she'd start crying again, Maggy simply nodded her head.

"Oh Mags," Cody said with a laugh, drawing her closer to him. "You're sweet, did you know that?" She pushed away from him, knowing that she had to put some distance between them, now, if only to protect her heart.

"I've let you down, Cody," she said softly, dropping her gaze to Bobby who was sleeping peacefully in her arms, blissfully unaware of what was going on.

"Oh Mags." Cody sighed heavily. "You haven't let me down, and you've got nothing to be sorry about."

"Yes, I do," she admitted dully, not daring to look at him. How could she tell him she was sorry she'd fallen in love with him when she wasn't sorry at all? Cody was the best thing that had ever happened to her. "Cody—I—I deliberately found fault with all those wom—"

"I know," Cody interrupted, his voice slightly amused.

"You knew?" she repeated blankly. "You knew I found fault with all those women?"

"I sure did," Cody said, throwing back his head and laughing at the look on her face.

"Shh," she cautioned, clamping one hand down over his mouth so he wouldn't wake Bobby. He kissed the palm of her hand softly, before pulling it away from his mouth.

"I guess I had an inkling that day at the theatrical agency. The day we ran into that pretty little blonde. What was her name?"

"Prissy Priscilla," Maggy said glumly, remembering the woman all too well.

"Prissy Priscilla," he said, raising his brows and looking as though he wondered where on earth Maggy had picked up the name. "I kind of figured it out when you told me her...mmm...*nose* was all wrong." His voice was full of humor and despite herself Maggy smiled weakly.

"I guess that wasn't too sensible," she grumbled, feeling a tad embarrassed.

"Not too logical or rational, either," he added gleefully, lifting his thumb to rub it slowly over her lips. "But I did think it was kind of cute. The way you hustled me out of that office, Mags. Your feet were moving so fast I thought the friction would set the carpet on fire." He chuckled softly, and Maggy's face turned crimson. She was grateful for the darkness, but she had a feeling Cody knew she was blushing to the tips of her ears.

"You're not mad?" she asked hesitantly.

"Does this face look mad?" he asked, cocking his head and giving her a wicked smile.

She looked at him for a long moment, her eyes going over every one of his handsome features. "No," she said softly. His face didn't look mad, in fact it looked wonderful. A clap of thunder boomed through the house, startling her. She held her breath as Bobby moaned softly. Maggy dropped a hand to smooth Bobby's hair, wanting to touch him, to have him feel safe and secure and know she was there. Squirming, Bobby whimpered softly, stuffed his thumb in his mouth, then settled himself more comfortably in her arms. She let her breath out slowly.

"Shh, Sport," Maggy whispered, gently rocking the child in her arms.

"You love him, don't you?" Cody asked, stroking her cheek gently.

"Yes." Maggy couldn't bring herself to look at Cody, fearing she'd start crying again. "I love him very much," she whispered. And I love you, too. Oh, Cody.

"He loves you, too, Mags," Cody said, his voice husky. "You know, honey, you've given that boy something his own mother never gave him." Cody paused to drop a soft kiss on her lips. "You've given him attention and affection. You're more of a mother than the woman who bore him. Mags, you've been wonderful with him. And," he added,

looking deeply into her eyes, "you've been wonderful to me."

Maggy shook her head. His words only added to
her pain. "No, I haven't, Cody. I promised to help
you, and I haven't. You've only got two days left
to find someone." Maggy sniffled and tried to wipe
her nose. "You kept your part of the bargain. You
taught me to have fun. I'm afraid I didn't keep mine,
though."

"Come on, Mags," Cody said, patting her back
and trying to reassure her. "It's not the end of the
world." Cody threaded his hands through her hair
and lifted her head so that she was forced to look at
him.

"But Cody, what about a woman? What about
Bobby's scholarship and the award cere—?" He
pressed a thumb to her lips to stop her.

"Mags, Mags, Mags," he said softly, shaking his
head. "Now you've got enough things to worry
about. Didn't you tell me you had a big shindig at
school tomorrow night?"

Maggy groaned. Oh Lord, she had forgotten about
Miss Barklay's faculty tea! The way she felt right
now, she didn't care if she ever saw Miss Barklay
or a cup of tea again.

"Yes, but Cody, what about—?" He pressed his
lips to hers to silence her.

"You let me worry about things. Come on now,
off to bed with you," he said abruptly, taking Bobby

from her arms and helping her to her feet. He didn't give her a chance to protest. "Come on, I'll walk you to your room, but only if you promise not to cry anymore, and," he added significantly, planting a kiss on her forehead, "if you promise not to worry."

"I promise," she lied, giving him what she hoped was a convincing smile. Even barefoot, Cody towered over her, and she was almost overwhelmed by his nearness. Laying an arm over her shoulders, Cody guided Maggy into the living room and up the stairs to her room.

"Now promise," he said sternly. "No more worrying, and no more tears. All right? I'll handle things." He tipped her chin up with one finger and her eyes met his. They stared at each other in silence, the only sound the howling of the wind as it swirled around the house. Maggy nodded as Cody's eyes darkened.

Wild anticipation raced through her for a moment before Cody's lips found hers. His mouth was soft, insistent as the hand that tipped her chin slid up to warm her cheek. His kiss deepened, tasting, savoring her. Maggy lifted a hand to his chest, and she felt the increased thud of his heart.

Bobby groaned suddenly, and they jumped apart guiltily. "Good night, Mags," Cody said softly.

"Good night," Maggy whispered, opening her door. She stopped and turned to him. "Cody, what are—?'' Maggy stopped. She wanted to know, to ask what he planned to do after the award ceremony. If he planned to go back home or what. But she couldn't bring herself to ask, fearing his answer.

"Mags?"

She gave him a watery smile. "Never mind. It was nothing. Good night, Cody."

"Good night, Mags."

Maggy fled into the safety of her room. Leaning against her closed door, Maggy let the tears come once again as she realized that although she loved Cody, there were more than just a few walls and rooms separating them. Climbing into bed, she cursed her fate, knowing they were separated by so much more.

"Miss Magee, did you hear me?"

"I'm sorry," Maggy said, rubbing her throbbing forehead and trying to direct her attention to the student who was sitting across from her desk. "What did you say, Miss...?" What was the girl's name? Maggy wondered, staring at the girl blankly.

"English," the girl supplied, looking at Maggy strangely. "Miss Magee, are you sure you're all right? Should I summon Miss Barklay?"

"No!" The word shot out of Maggy's mouth, startling the student, and the girl sat up abruptly. The last person Maggy wanted to see right now was her boss. She was exhausted from lack of sleep and terribly out of sorts. She had lain awake all night, worrying despite her promise to Cody not to. This morning when she'd come down to breakfast, Cody and Bobby were gone. All she'd found had been a note, saying he would see her tonight. Frustrated and worried about Cody and Bobby's whereabouts, Maggy couldn't seem to think of anything else. Where had he gone? They had spent nearly every waking moment together the past weeks, and for him to just leave, well, she didn't know what to make of it. She was worried sick. Worried that he was gone and that he might not return. She pushed the thought to the back of her mind.

Today had been one big blur, and Maggy knew she still had to face the faculty tea. Sighing heavily, Maggy tried to redirect her attention to Miss... English and her problem.

"I'm sorry," Maggy said with a smile. "Now why don't you tell me again why you were sent to my office."

The girl fidgeted in her chair, clearly uncomfortable at being sent to the assistant headmistress's office. "I was reading a book in English class."

"Excuse me?" Maggy returned, looking at the girl blankly. Since when was reading in English class a reason to be sent to her office? Her office was the place where minor and some major infractions were handled before the students were sent on to Miss Barklay.

The young girl shifted in her chair, crossing and uncrossing her knee-socked legs. "Miss Magee," she said at last, her words coming out in a rush. "I was reading *Love's Sweet Honor*. I couldn't help it. I just had to see how it ended. It's just the most romantic book." The girl sighed heavily, her face dreamy. "The heroine, her name is Celeste, she dies in the end, and..." Her voice trailed off and she glanced down self-consciously at the scuffed toe of her shoe. "I guess *Love's Sweet Honor* is not on the recommended—"

"Reading list for this semester," Maggy finished for her. Smiling, Maggy stood up and rounded her desk, coming to rest on one corner in front of the girl. "Miss English—" Maggy looked at the girl, really looked at her. She was young, about fourteen, and extremely pretty with wide-set blue eyes and long blond hair caught up behind her head as the rules at Miss Avalon's dictated. "What is your first name?" Maggy asked abruptly and the girl looked stunned. All of the students at Miss Avalon's Academy were *always* addressed by their proper, formal names. "Your first name?" Maggy prompted gently, and the girl smiled shyly.

"Rebecca. But my friends call me Becky."

"Becky," Maggy said softly and the girl's smile widened. "I understand how *Love's Sweet Honor* could capture your attention and imagination. I, too, have gotten caught up in a book." Maggy remembered the day she had been caught reading Cody's book. "One that was not on the recommended reading list, either," Maggy whispered conspiratorially. "So I can understand how it can happen. But wouldn't it be better if you did your reading in the privacy of your room?"

"My room?" the girl echoed, clearly shocked at the idea. Even the students' rooms and their contents were subject to the rules and regulations of the academy, not to mention Miss Barklay's inspections.

"Yes, I'm sure you'll be able to discover a... discreet place to store your books," Maggy suggested with a lift of her brow.

"Oh yes, Miss Magee," the girl returned happily. "I'm sure I can."

"Good." Maggy nodded, and came to her feet. "I think you can return to class now."

"That's it? No extra chores?" The girl clearly looked perplexed.

"No," Maggy said with a laugh. "I don't think *Love's Sweet Honor* warrants any extra chores. You may return to class."

"Thank you." Becky jumped from her chair and bounced toward the door, clearly relieved at getting off so easily. "Miss Magee?" She stopped at the door and turned to look at Maggy.

"Yes, Becky?"

"You know, I was really scared when I got sent

down here. A lot of the girls said you were..."
Becky stopped, and a flush crept over her face.

"A lot of the girls said I was what?" Maggy
asked, her voice soft.

"Well, they sometimes call you Miss Meany, instead of Miss Magee, because they say you're almost as mean and stuffy as Miss Barklay." Maggy's
heart constricted at the girl's words, but she carefully kept her face blank. "But you're not," Becky
said firmly, a smile on her face. "You're nice.
And," she added softly, "you're pretty."

"Thank you, Becky," Maggy said, feeling
touched by the girl's words. "Now you'd better get
to class."

Maggy reclaimed her chair and thought about
Becky's words. So the students at the academy
called her Miss Meany. The idea hurt, but Maggy
wondered why she should be surprised. In the past
she had been as rigid and stuffy as Miss Barklay,
and just as staunch and unbending in enforcing the
rules and regulations of the school.

So what if Becky had been caught reading the
latest, hottest romance novel? What was wrong with
that? The girl was at an age when love and romance
were not only an intriguing mystery, but uppermost
in her mind. It was a natural thing for her to be
curious, and to try to quench her curiosity.

Her infraction was hardly a criminal offense. But

just a few weeks ago, Maggy knew that she would've seen it differently.

Staring off into space, Maggy sighed deeply and swiveled around in her chair to stare out the window.

So the students thought of her as a clone of Miss Barklay. A month ago that would have pleased her, made her feel as if she were doing her job and living up to her boss's expectations.

But now, today, it only made her feel sad. Did she want to go through life with a reputation as a stern mistress whose life was governed only by the academy and its rules and regulations?

Was that *all* she really wanted out of life? Cody's image flashed before her eyes, and without a doubt Maggy knew that the academy wasn't all she wanted to settle for. Was she willing to settle just for crumbs? She didn't know anymore. Maggy sat staring out her window, torn between her love for Cody and Bobby and her job.

If she gave in now, she'd throw it all away—her job, her career, everything—for a man she'd known less than a month. For a man who was her opposite in every single way. For a man… Tears filled her eyes. Oh Lord, for a man she was totally and hopelessly in love with. For a man who filled her days with fun and laughter and made her feel really alive.

Her head knew all the reasons she shouldn't do anything irresponsible or irrational, but her heart didn't. All her heart knew was that it was filled with love for an outrageous man and an elfin little boy. All her heart knew was that if she didn't do... something, she was going to lose both of them.

Could she let her heart overrule her head?

Maggy sat for a long time until she had her answer. She wanted more than rules and regulations in her life. She wanted Cody and Bobby!

Maggy couldn't wait to tell Cody, but first she had to find him!

Chapter Nine

"**M**other, are you sure you haven't heard from Cody?" Maggy continued to pace the length of the living room as she spoke.

"Dear." Elizabeth sighed, then looked up from the evening newspaper. "You've asked me that at least twenty times since you came home. Now *read my lips*. I have not heard from Cody or Bobby. I'm sure they'll be back soon. Please stop worrying. And please stop pacing; you're going to wear a hole in my favorite Oriental."

"I'm sorry, Mother." Maggy continued to pace. "But I'm so worried about them. Where could they be?"

"Maggy, be sensible. You're all worked up over nothing. I'm sure they're fine."

"But Mother—"

"Maggy, please?" Elizabeth smiled gently. "He'll be back, I'm sure of it. Now please calm yourself."

Maggy glanced at her watch. "I can't wait for him any longer. If I don't leave now I'm going to be late for the faculty tea."

"You're not really going out dressed like…that, are you?"

Maggy came to an abrupt halt and glanced down at herself in bewilderment. Her formfitting navy tea-length silk dress fell in billowing folds around her ankles. High-heeled pumps in the same shade of navy completed her outfit. She had piled her blond tresses atop her head and fastened matching navy and silver combs amidst the curls. Miss Barklay's teas were formal affairs, and Maggy felt that the quiet elegance of her dress was more than appropriate to the circumstances.

"Dressed like what, Mother?" she inquired.

"Dressed in that dreary old thing!" her mother said with a frown.

"Mother, you know very well how stuffy and formal these affairs are—"

"*Affairs!*" Elizabeth chortled, drawing the word out and giving it a great deal more significance than necessary. "Dear," she said slowly. "Miss Barklay wouldn't know an *affair* if it walked up and bit her

on her pointy little nose. And as for your dress, con-
victs wear cheerier outfits.''

"Mother, please.'' Maggy sighed and pressed a
hand to her forehead. She was worried sick and in
no mood for her mother's barbs—or Miss Barklay's
tea for that matter. With a heartfelt sigh, Maggy
knew she was going to have to put up with both of
them that evening.

Her mother abruptly stood up. "Sure you don't
want to borrow my sneakers?'' Elizabeth waggled
her feet, which were adorned with her neon-green
glow-in-the-dark tennis shoes. "It sure would add
some life to that outfit.''

Maggy bit back a smile, and picked up her evening bag from the telephone table. Her mother was
incorrigible, but she loved her dearly. "Thank you,
Mother, but no. I think I'll simply have to suffer
through the evening in my plain navy pumps.''

"Suffer is right,'' her mother grumbled under her
breath. Elizabeth looked thoughtful for a moment.
"How about my colored pop beads? Chester seemed
to like them.''

"Chester?'' Maggy repeated with a lift of her
brow. "Mother,'' she said cautiously. "Who is
Chester?''

"Chester,'' her mother repeated vaguely, waving
her hand in the air as if that explained everything.

Maggy looked at her mother carefully. "Don't tell

me you mean *Mayor* Chesterfield?'' she cried in alarm.

''Why of course, dear,'' her mother answered, picking up her newspaper again and burying her nose in it. ''He really did like my beads. In fact, we have a date tonight; we're going bike riding.'' Her mother flashed her a sultry wink. ''I promised Chester I'd wear them. He just *loves* the sound of those beads popping.'' Elizabeth sighed dreamily and Maggy's smile grew wider. Evidently all her worrying about her mother and the mayor had been for nothing. It sounded as though Cody had been right about the mayor, she mused, knowing Cody had been right about a great many other things.

''Mother, I'm leaving now. Please try to stay out of trouble,'' she admonished with a laugh, bending to plant a kiss on her mother's cheek. ''And if you hear from Cody, *please* let me know immediately.'' If she didn't hurry, she was going to be late for Miss Barklay's tea. And that, she knew, was an unpardonable offense. ''I'm really worried about him,'' Maggy added softly. Her mother's eyes met hers for a moment, and Elizabeth smiled.

''Don't worry, dear,'' she said gently, patting Maggy's arm. ''I'm sure all is well.''

That, Maggy realized as she drove toward the academy, was simply a matter of opinion. How could all be well when she hadn't seen Cody or Bobby in almost twenty-four hours?

Last night when she had sobbed her heart out on Cody's shoulder, she'd admitted that she'd deliberately found fault with all the women prospects they had interviewed. Had Cody decided to find one on his own? The thought caused Maggy's nerves to tighten in fear. She had so much to tell him; every moment that passed made her all the bolder. She had to find Cody, had to tell him what she'd decided. She had to tell him that she was ready to let her heart rule her head.

Pulling into the academy parking lot, Maggy grabbed her bag and hurried inside, her mind full of Cody.

"Margaret!"

Miss Barklay's voice rang through the air and Maggy stifled a groan. Despite her personal problems and her worries, she had a responsibility to her boss tonight. Tonight, perhaps for the last time, she was Miss Margaret Magee, assistant headmistress of Miss Avalon's Academy for Young Ladies.

Forcing a bright smile, Maggy moved through the crowded room, and headed toward Miss Barklay, who was talking to a large, distinguished-looking man.

"Margaret, I'd like you to meet Senator English. I'm sure you remember his daughter, Rebecca?" Miss Barklay's inflection indicated that Maggy should remember the girl, not for her name or her father's political standing, but for her infraction of the rules.

Maggy smiled and extended her hand. "Senator, it's a pleasure to meet you. Your daughter Rebecca is a lovely young woman."

"Why, thank you, Miss Magee," Senator English replied, smiling as he took her hand. "Becky is quite fond of you, too. As a matter of fact, she's spoken quite highly of you." He glanced at Miss Barklay and a congenial smile lit his face. "It seems you two have similar tastes in literature?"

She knew he was speaking of his daughter's contraband book—and her own. Aware of Miss Barklay's probing eyes, Maggy returned his smile, instantly liking the man. "Yes," she said with a laugh. "I guess we do."

"Miss Magee," he said sincerely. "I understand your credentials are impeccable. If you ever decide to leave Miss Avalon's, please give me a call. I'm head of a committee that's currently funding an experimental project that will hire capable educators to serve as full-time consultants to students preparing for college. It's my belief that in addition to a good basic education, students need a comprehensive program in order to pass the rigid tests required to get into a top-flight college."

"Senator," Miss Barklay interrupted sharply. "I'm sure Miss Magee appreciates your offer, but she has a very bright future here at Miss Avalon's.

Don't you, Margaret?'' Miss Barklay's eyes were dark, and she was quite clearly annoyed that the Senator was trying to steal one of her staff out from under her nose.

"Thank you, Senator," Maggy said, feeling genuinely flattered at the man's offer. "That's very kind of you. I'll keep it in mind."

"Come along, Margaret, we have other guests to attend to." Miss Barklay grasped Maggy's elbow and steered her away from the senator, but not before he flashed Maggy a wink. Maggy smiled.

"Margaret," Miss Barklay said as she dragged Maggy across the room. "I'd like you to meet Wadsworth Wellington. He is our new English instructor."

Maggy turned, anxious to meet the man who thought *Love's Sweet Honor* was worth a trip to her office.

Maggy's eyes widened, and she stifled a smile. The man had the posture of a fishhook, the face of an apple left in the cellar too long, rheumy green eyes, and clearly not a romantic bone in his entire little body.

"Mr. Wellington."

"Margaret," he said with a flourish, extending a long, bony hand in her direction. Maggy took his hand. "And it's *Professor* Wellington," he clarified.

"Professor, it's a pleasure to meet you," Maggy

muttered, trying to extract her hand from his, which
was cold and clammy.

"Actually, I'm not really an *English* instructor,"
he confided, dipping his head toward her. "I've a
Ph.D. in Linguistics." His green eyes widened in
delight. "Language is my passion. In fact words are
the prevalent overlying factor in the social organi-
zation of humanity." Maggy nodded her head
blankly, glancing around the room as the man went
on. "Really, Margaret, language's true existence is
not so much in the printed word, but in the sense
of...community. Any disintegration of the commu-
nity, whether geographical or by class differentia-
tion, will cause distinct changes in the pattern of all
of our words and languages. Don't you agree?"

"Excuse me?" Maggy looked at him again, her
mind whirling. Was this how she wanted to spend
the rest of her life? Surrounded by pompous intel-
lectuals who vied with each other to see who could
be the most boring? Living her life boxed into a little
room labeled Rules and Regulations?

"I say, Margaret, weren't you listening to me?"

Maggy looked up at the professor, and a bright
smile appeared on her lips. She knew without a
doubt that this was *not* how she wanted to spend her
life, and the professor, bless his unromantic heart,
had just confirmed it.

Miss Avalon's Academy for Young Ladies was a
wonderful place, but it wasn't for Maggy. Not any-

more. There was a whole world out there waiting for her. Miss Avalon's was her past. Now she knew that Bobby and Cody were her future.

"Professor." Maggy laughed, throwing her arms around the startled man and planting a kiss on his cheek. "I was listening to you. In fact, I heard every word you said, and even a few that you didn't. Thank you," she gushed, kissing him again. "Thank you!"

"Margaret," the professor stammered, freeing himself from her embrace and blushing down to the knot of his bobbing Adam's apple. "Please, control yourself. This is hardly the time or the place." He darted a glance around. "Meet me later at my place," he whispered.

The front door screeched open and the well-modulated hum of the crowd subsided to a startled hush. It was like watching a slow-motion movie as all eyes turned toward the door.

"Mags!" Cody burst into the room with Bobby on his hip and her mother on his heels.

"Cody!" Maggy cried, pushing past the all-too-interested professor and the rest of the assembled faculty.

"Where have you been?" she demanded and Cody and Bobby exchanged glances. How could a simple little glance look so guilty, she wondered?

"Ma-ma," Bobby cried, trying to climb out of Cody's arms to get to her.

"Oh, Cody! Bobby!" Maggy threw her arms around the two of them, hugging them tightly, oblivious to the horrified gasps that surrounded her. "I'm so glad to see you!" She had lived in fear that Cody and Bobby had left her life. She had so much to tell Cody.

"Ma-ma," Bobby cooed, winding his chubby arms around her neck and clinging to her. Maggy kissed him soundly on the cheek.

"Hi, Sport," she whispered, giving him another kiss.

"I told you all was well, dear," Elizabeth said with a smile. Maggy's eyes rounded at the sight of her mother's attire. It was a far cry from the outfit she'd had on when Maggy left the house. Elizabeth was now dressed in brown leather knee britches and—despite the oppressive heat—she wore a matching leather bomber jacket. On her head sat a leather aviator cap and goggles. Small tufts of gray hair escaped from under the earflaps of her cap, giving her mother the appearance of a blooming tulip. Her feet were adorned with her neon-green running shoes, and she had Chester's favorite pop beads looped around her neck.

"Nice outfit, Mother," Maggy commented with a smile. "But don't you think it's a bit warm for bike riding?"

"Depends on what kind of bike we're talking about." Elizabeth's eyes twinkled with delight.

"Uh-oh," she announced. "Here comes the dragon lady."

"Margaret!" Miss Barklay marched up to them, her face red with anger. "What is the meaning of this? Who on earth are these—?"

"Mother." Maggy frowned, ignoring Miss Barklay. "What do you mean it depends on what kind of bike riding? Just what kind of bike riding are we talking about?"

"Mags," Cody broke in, bending to whisper in her ear. "I have to talk to you. *Now.* It's important." Cody grabbed her elbow in an effort to guide her toward the door, but Miss Barklay clamped a hand on her other arm.

"Margaret! What on earth is the meaning of this? Who are these people? And where are you going?"

Cody stopped abruptly and turned his attention to the stunned headmistress. "You must be Miss Barklay," he said with a smile, grabbing her hand and pumping wildly. "I'm Wild Bill Cody. It's a pleasure to finally meet you, ma'am. I need to borrow Mags here for a moment, but we'll be right back." He plucked Bobby free of Maggy's arms. "This here's Bobby. Could you keep an eye on him for a minute?" Not giving the woman a chance to answer, Cody plopped the squirming toddler into Miss Barklay's arms.

"Oh my!" Miss Barklay whimpered. She stared down her pointy nose at Bobby, and the child puckered up and blew a loud, wet raspberry right into her stunned face.

"Mags, let's go." Cody grabbed Maggy's hand and headed for the door.

"Where have you been all day?" Maggy asked once they were outside. "I was so worried."

"That's what I have to talk to you about," Cody said, slowly backing Maggy up against the dimly lit stone wall of Avalon Hall. "God, I missed you," he whispered, dropping a quick kiss on her lips.

"Oh, Cody." Maggy tightened her arms around his neck.

"Mags, honey, listen." Cody lifted his hand to cradle her face. "You don't have to worry about finding a woman for me anymore."

"I know," she said with a wicked smile.

"You know?" Cody frowned at her. "How do you know?"

"Because," she said softly, wrapping her arms around him. "*I'm* going to accept the award for you."

Cody stared down at her. "What!"

Maggy's smile grew broader. "*I said I'm going to accept the award for you.*"

"Come on, Mags, you know you can't do that."

"Yes I can. Oh, Cody." Sighing, Maggy pressed her temples against his chest. "I've got so much to tell you. I've done a lot of thinking and I realize now that everything you said was true. I *was* settling for crumbs in my life. Since I met you and Bobby, my life has changed.'' Maggy stopped and looked up into his eyes. ''Cody, Bobby's future is just as important to me as it is to you.''

''But Mags,'' he protested. ''What about your job? Your career?''

''Cody, my career is still important to me, but I realized that while it's important it's not the only thing in my life, not anymore. You've taught me so much.'' She smiled. ''Cody, you've shown me that life can be fun. It doesn't always have to be rigid and uncompromising. You've given me something I never had before, the confidence to be myself. I guess maybe that's why I just accepted my life before, just accepted the strict boundaries set for me by my position. I was hiding behind my job, Cody, hiding away from life. I don't want to do that anymore,'' she whispered softly, tears welling up in her eyes.

''No, Mags, that's not true.'' He shook his head. ''I shouldn't have said those things, Mags. I had no right.''

''You had every right, Cody. If it wasn't for you...'' Maggy's voice faded as her heart filled with love.

''Oh, Mags,'' he said softly, gathering her close again. ''Last night, honey, when I saw how pained you were about finding me a woman, well, I finally realized just how hard it's been for you. I know you never liked the idea to begin with, and I know the only reason you agreed to help me was to keep your mother out of trouble.''

''Cody, that's not true. That's not the only reason.'' She cursed the day at the pool when Cody had asked her why she was helping him, and she had lied, telling him that keeping her mother out of trouble was the only reason. Why hadn't she told him the truth?

''That first night, when your mom and I got arrested, I should have just taken Bobby and hightailed it back home. But I couldn't. I was drawn to you from the moment I laid eyes on you. I can't bear to see you so torn up like you were last night, knowing I was the cause. I knew you thought what I wanted to do wasn't sensible, logical or—''

''Rational,'' she supplied, looking up into his eyes and wondering why he looked so sad.

''Yeah, well, I knew last night I couldn't hold you to a promise that goes against everything you believe in. It was wrong and unfair of me, and—''

''Oh, Cody,'' she whispered, taking his face in her hands.

''No,'' he said sharply, pulling away. ''Let me finish. Maggy, I've never done a damn sensible thing in my life. But it's not too late to start. I can't let you throw away everything you've worked for. Don't you see, honey, being headmistress was your dream. I can't steal your dream from you. I just can't. If I let you do this for me, if I let you accept this award, someday I know you'll regret it. I'm grateful for the offer, Mags, you'll never know how much it means to me. I'm very grateful, but I just can't let you do that." He smiled suddenly and touched her face.

No! The desperate cry echoed in Maggy's mind, and she shivered as her stricken eyes met his.

"I appreciate all you've done for Bobby. Honey, he loves you more than anything in this world. Don't think I don't know how hard it was for you to come to this decision." He sighed and dragged a hand through his hair. "You're one very special lady. But I can't and won't let you do it. You deserve more, Mags, so much more."

Maggy's chest constricted with pain. Deserved? She stared at Cody with eyes blinded by tears. Stubbornly she blinked them back. Cody didn't love her. He was grateful and appreciative, but it wasn't love. Not the way she loved him. How could she have been so blind?

She had expected Cody to be thrilled and overjoyed at her offer. Apparently he wasn't. He was grateful and appreciative, but she didn't want his gratitude, she wanted his love!

Tears of humiliation burned her eyes; Maggy stubbornly blinked them away as she stepped out of Cody's arms. What a fool she had been! She was willing to sacrifice everything for him, to let her

heart rule her head, and Cody had turned her down.
Rejected her. How could she love him so much and
not have her love returned? He couldn't love her
and hurt her like this. Nothing had ever hurt like
this.

"Now, honey, Bobby and I have to leave tonight.
That's what I came here to tell you. I've hired Priscilla and she's going to accept the award for me.
We've got a lot to do before the ceremony tomorrow
night. I just came back to get our stuff." Cody
grabbed her tightly around the waist, pressing her
close to him. "I want you to come to the award
ceremony. *Promise me, now?*" he whispered
fiercely. "Promise me!"

"I promise," she whispered hoarsely. Cody gathered her up in his arms again, crushing her to him.
With a wordless cry, Maggy went willingly, knowing it would probably be the last time she ever held
Cody in her arms. She clung to him, holding on to
him tightly, trying to memorize the feel of him in
her arms.

"Mags," Cody said, finally releasing her. "I have
to go now." He bent to kiss her brow. "Are you all
right?"

She looked up at him. All right? He was walking
out of her life and he wanted to know if she was all
right?

Maggy nodded solemnly. She didn't think she
would ever be all right again.

"Good. Mags, I'm sorry, but I've got to run. Bobby and I are driving back into Chicago tonight. Do you want to come in and say goodbye to him?"

Maggy shook her head. "I'll see him tomorrow," she lied, knowing she would never see either of them again. If she had to say goodbye to Cody *and* Bobby now, she'd fall apart.

"Bye, Mags." Cody pressed a quick kiss on her brow, then turned and headed back inside. Wordlessly Maggy watched him, loving him.

Cody and Bobby were gone from her life as quickly as they had entered it. A sob caught in her throat and Maggy sagged against the wall, letting the tears finally come.

Great racking sobs shook her body, and Maggy cried until she had no more tears. How ironic, she thought, dabbing at her face. How utterly ironic that the first time she let her heart rule her head— Maggy pressed a hand to her throbbing temples, unable to bear thinking about it.

Perhaps it was better this way, she reflected, trying to stifle a fresh flood of tears. Cody had found the woman he needed, Bobby was going to get his scholarship, and Cody's bosses at Adventure Publications were going to be pleased. All of Cody's problems were solved. Cody was going back to his world, and she would be left with hers.

Her world.

Pulling herself upright, Maggy glanced around at

the familiar grounds of Avalon Academy. Once upon a time all of this had been enough, but that was before a handsome, outrageous rogue had drowned her in his charm and stolen her heart.

I don't have a right to steal your dreams, Cody had said. But without knowing it, that was exactly what he'd done. *He* was her dream.

"I love you, Cody," she whispered, knowing he couldn't hear her. *Oh, Cody, I love you.*

the, melling control of a world threatering. Once
upon a time all of this had seen trouble, but that
as before, a number of vengeance came. Had
survived it in the thing and the let her plan
hismel she is ashiman until she is trouble. Cody
had said they will not automatedly, they will always
when a change it was all trouble asked
I was young, cody we was when son, knowing he
could train him Out One a show when....

Chapter Ten

"Dear, I think Chester and I will go skinny-
dipping this afternoon."

"That's nice, Mother," Maggy said, not bother-
ing to look up from the uneaten eggs she'd been
pushing around her plate. "Have a good time." The
house was so silent without Cody and Bobby. The
sudden stillness was about to drive her crazy.

Frowning, Elizabeth leaned over and patted
Maggy's arms. "Dear, I'm worried about you."

"What?" Maggy looked up to find her mother
watching her intently. "Why are you worried about
me?" Boy, this was a switch. She was usually the
one worrying about her mother.

"I just told you I was going *skinny-dipping* and
you told me to have a good time." Elizabeth looked

at her shrewdly. "Maggy, what happened between you and Cody last night?"

Cody...

Maggy glanced down at her plate as her eyes brimmed with tears. Her heart ached and shattered at the thought of Cody. He had to go and she had to stay and that's the way things were to be. He couldn't change who he was, and she realized now—too late—she didn't want him to change. She was the one who had changed, but she realized sadly that was too late, too.

Maggy closed her eyes as the pain tore through her. She'd never even had the chance to tell him she loved him. Not that it mattered now. Perhaps it was better this way, she reasoned, knowing in her heart that it wasn't. Perhaps it was better to get it over with, to have him and Bobby walk out of her life now, before she fell any deeper in love with them.

"Dear?" Elizabeth touched her arm gently and Maggy raised her eyes to her mother's.

"Oh, Mother," she moaned, letting the tears fall. "I've made such a mess of things." Her mother came around the table and cradled Maggy in her arms.

"Shh, honey, don't cry." Her mother was silent for a moment. "You love him, don't you?" Elizabeth asked, and Maggy nodded her head, wiping away her tears. "Did you tell him, dear?"

Maggy laughed shortly. "No, I never got a

chance. Ever since Cody arrived—well—I've been doing a lot of thinking about my life, and last night I told Cody I was going to accept the award for him—''

"Well, good for you, dear, good for you! It's about time you let your heart rule your head." Her mother's words brought on a fresh outbreak of tears, and Maggy shook her head.

"I wish it were that simple. Cody turned me down." Maggy sniffled harder. "He said he couldn't let me give up everything I'd worked for. That I deserved more. Cody said he couldn't live with himself if I lost my job because of him." She raised her tear-soaked face to her mother's. "He already hired someone else."

"I see," her mother said softly, stroking her hair. "That explains a lot, doesn't it?"

"It doesn't explain anything," Maggy sniffled, and pushed away her untouched plate.

Elizabeth laughed softly. "Honey, don't you see? It explains everything. Cody loves you. He's not about to let you do something you might regret later on. Why, he probably feels that if you did accept the award and then lost your job—a job that's meant so much to you, why you might come to resent him someday. Cody's a very special man, dear. While he might not live his life according to anyone else's rules, he knows *you* do. He's not about to have you take such a risk for him. You think you're willing to do it now, but later you might not feel the same. Cody's afraid to take that chance. He's a proud man, dear, and a good one.''

''But Mother, I told Cody last night that I've finally realized that Miss Avalon's isn't the *only* place for me. I love what I do, but there are other positions for me, other avenues to explore. I no longer want the kind of job that requires twenty-four-hour dedication, or one that I have to adapt my whole life to. That's the whole point, Mother. I want something else in my life. I want the kind of job that allows me *to have a life*. I know that now.'' Maggy looked up at her mother. ''What am I going to do?''

Elizabeth stood up. ''Well, dear, that depends on what you want out of life. You're the only one who can decide that.''

''I want Cody and Bobby.''

''Then give him a chance,'' Elizabeth said softly. ''He loves you, you know. And so does Bobby.''

Maggy jumped up from the table and kissed her mother's cheek. ''Mother, you're right.''

''Wait a minute, dear. Where are you going? You didn't even eat your breakfast. And what about the award ceremony?''

''I'm not hungry,'' Maggy called, pushing the door open and scooping up her purse. ''We've got plenty of time. You get ready and I'll meet you back here. Right now I've got to get to school. There's a little matter at the academy that needs attending to.''

* * *

"But Margaret, surely you can't be serious?" Hands clasped tightly together, Miss Barklay was planted in the middle of Maggy's office, watching in horror as she cleaned out her desk.

"I'm very serious," Maggy said with a smile. "I've loved working at the academy, Miss Barklay. I really have. But it's time to move on."

"It's Senator English, isn't it?" Miss Barklay demanded. "He's lured you away with his job offer. I knew I shouldn't have invited that man."

Maggy laughed softly. "No, Miss Barklay, it's not Senator English. No one lured me into anything." She glanced up and smiled. "As a matter of fact, I don't even have another job."

"Then why are you resigning? I don't understand." Miss Barklay narrowed her eyes, looking down her nose at Maggy. "This is hardly a sensible move, Margaret. It's not like you to do something so irrational. You're giving up a very safe, secure job with a promising future for absolutely no reason. Are you sure you're feeling all right?"

Maggy laughed, scooping up the box of her belongings and tucking it under her arm. "I'm feeling fine. In fact I never felt better. Leaving the academy after so many years is difficult." Maggy glanced around her office. "I'm going to miss this place. And you," she added softly. Despite Miss Barklay's rigid ways, Maggy knew the woman was only doing what she thought best for the academy. But now it was time for Maggy to do what she thought best for herself. "But it's time."

"This has something to do with that Wild man, the one that disrupted my faculty tea last night, doesn't it?" Miss Barklay sighed heavily. "Margaret, how on earth did you ever get involved with someone like *him*?"

Maggy smiled dreamily. "It really doesn't have anything to do with Cody. It has to do with how I want to live my life. I've finally realized that there is more to life than just the academy, and now I want to find out what I've been missing." She walked around her desk and stood in front of Miss Barklay. It was going to be hard to leave this place after so many years, but Maggy felt no regrets. She knew in her heart that it was the right thing to do.

"Margaret." Miss Barklay looked forlorn. "I guess in a way I do understand. You're young, and you've never really seen or experienced much of life except within the walls of Avalon. I envy you. When I was young, I too had an opportunity to—" Miss Barklay flushed. "There was a young man, and he—I—" Miss Barklay seized Maggy in a tight hug. "I wish you well, Margaret. And I hope you and your young man—I hope your life is happy."

Tears filled Maggy's eyes, and she dropped a kiss on Miss Barklay's cheek. "Thank you," she whispered, returning the older woman's hug. "Thank you."

Miss Barklay straightened and dabbed at her eyes. "I guess I'll say goodbye now. Stay well, Margaret," Miss Barklay said softly. "Stay well."

Nodding, Maggy headed for the door, feeling an inner peace she hadn't felt in a long, long time.

"Margaret?" Maggy turned. "Do you think—I mean could you—" Miss Barklay drew herself up, a faint smile on her lips. "Do you think," she whispered, "you could get me a copy of your book?"

"My book?" Maggy repeated with a frown.

"Yes, you know, *Wild Bill Cody's Amazing Adventures of the Amazon*?"

Laughing softly, Maggy nodded. "I'll be happy to. And I'll even get it autographed for you." After one last glance around, Maggy turned and walked through the doorway, her step light, her spirits soaring. One part of her life was ending. But another was just beginning.

"Do you see him, Mother?" Following an usher down the center aisle, Maggy craned her neck and looked around the crowded auditorium.

"Here you are." The usher pointed to two empty seats in the front row.

"Mother," Maggy said softly, taking her seat. "I don't see Cody or Bobby." She frowned. "Nor Priscilla for that matter." She raised her head to look around again.

Her mother patted her hand. "I'm sure they're here, dear, don't worry."

The lights dimmed and a hush fell over the crowd as a neatly dressed woman walked across the stage and took her place behind the podium. Maggy shifted restlessly in her seat, wondering and worrying about Cody. Surely he wouldn't miss the award ceremony. So where was he? Fear tripped her heart. Maybe something had happened with Priscilla; maybe she'd backed out at the last minute. Another thought entered Maggy's mind, and she shuddered. Oh Lord, maybe something happened to Cody and Bobby! She knew how important this was to him, knew there was no way he would miss the ceremony unless something was wrong. Her heart began to beat in double time, and her palms grew moist with fear.

"Ladies and gentlemen," the woman began. "My name is Alice Spenser, and I'm the editor of *Modern Motherhood*. I'd like to thank all of you for coming to *Modern Motherhood*'s tenth annual Mother of the Year Award Ceremony. This year is a bit different than other years; the winner of this year's Mother of the Year contest *isn't a mother*." A low rumble of laughter rippled through the audience and Maggy sat up straighter. Oh Lord, maybe they'd found out about Priscilla. Maybe the editor knew that Priscilla wasn't a mother.

"Well," Alice went on with a little laugh after

the noise had died down. "Perhaps I should say the winner is not a mother in the…traditional sense. I'm sure you're all a little anxious to find out exactly what I'm talking about. So without further ado I'd like to present *Modern Motherhood*'s 1988 winner of the Mother of the Year award, Mr. William Cody."

There was a moment of stunned silence from the crowd and Maggy gasped as a smiling Cody, holding Bobby by the hand, walked out on stage. The applause was thunderous, and Maggy reached for Elizabeth's hand.

"Oh, Mother," she breathed, watching as Cody swung Bobby up on his hip and took his place behind the podium. "What is he doing?" Maggy knew what he was doing, but didn't know why. Cody looked wonderful. He was wearing a three-piece gray pin-striped suit, while Bobby was dressed in knee britches and a blue sport coat with matching bow tie. Wide-eyed, Bobby looked around the dark auditorium, clinging tightly to Cody's neck.

"Ladies and gentlemen," Cody began, his eyes searching the crowd. Maggy knew the instant he spotted her, for his eyes lit with amusement and he flashed her a grin. "My name is Wild Bill Cody, and I'm honored to accept the 1988 Mother of the Year award. Now, I know I don't look like a traditional mother." He grinned. "I'm a bit hairier than most." He waited for the laughter to die down before he continued. "But nevertheless I am indeed Bobby's mother. And father. When I first learned I had won this award, I admit I was a little scared. I'm a writer and I write all kinds of things, including a series of action and adventure books that some of you might have heard of." There was a loud burst of applause, acknowledging Cody's books, and Maggy's heart filled with joy. She was so proud of him.

"Now don't get me wrong. I'm very, very proud and honored to have won this award. But I was afraid if I accepted the award in person—if my readers learned that Wild Bill Cody had won a mothering award... Well, I was worried that I might lose credibility. In fact, I was so worried about it, I had every intention of hiring a woman to represent me and accept the award." Cody paused, and his eyes found Maggy's. He was speaking to the crowd, but Maggy had a feeling he was talking just to her.

"But something happened to change my mind. Someone very special taught me that sometimes you have to let your heart rule your head, and let the consequences be damned. This wonderful lady was willing to sacrifice everything—her job, her career, everything she's worked for so that *I* wouldn't lose any credibility, and so that my son here wouldn't lose his scholarship." Cody looked across the audience. "I guess to me that's what motherhood is all about. Giving birth doesn't make you a mother.

What makes you a mother is giving unselfishly, putting a child's needs before your own. How you treat and love a child, well, that's what motherhood's all about. It doesn't matter if you're the birth mother or the birth father. Anyone can give birth, but it takes a special person to be a real mother. Now, this lady I'm talking about—she's never had a child, but no one could be more of a mother to my boy here.''

''Oh, Cody,'' Maggy whispered as tears filled her eyes.

''In fact her offer was so generous, so unselfish that it started me thinking. If she had been willing to risk everything and accept this award to insure my son's future, then how could I do any less?'' Cody shifted his frame, his eyes on Maggy. ''That's why I decided to proudly and happily accept this award myself.''

Maggy sprang to her feet, leading the thunderous applause as Alice Spenser crossed the stage to present Cody with his plaque.

The crowd pressed toward Cody, making it impossible for Maggy to get to him. Bulbs flashed as the photographers and reporters vied for his attention.

Startled by all the attention and noise, Bobby began to cry. Maggy pushed her way through the crowd and climbed the stairs to the stage. Bobby and Cody spotted her at the same time.

''Mags,'' Cody whispered, his eyes filled with

love. She walked right into his arms. "Oh, Mags," he murmured softly, pressing his lips to her neck. "I was so afraid you wouldn't come. I love you, Mags. I love you."

"Oh, Cody." Maggy held him tight, her eyes brimming with tears. "I love you, too."

Squashed between the two of them, Bobby started to wail. "Down! Now, down!"

Cody slid his lips from Maggy's, and smiled at her. "I have to tend to a few things here, but will you wait for me?"

"Forever," she whispered, knowing she'd been waiting for him her whole life. Cody was her dream, her love, her everything.

"Ma-ma," Bobby cried, as another flashbulb went off in his face.

"Come here, Sport," Maggy said, taking the weeping child out of Cody's arms and snuggling him close. She had missed these two so. "I love you, Cody," she breathed, leaning forward to kiss him again. "You finish here. We'll wait for you behind the stage."

"Promise you'll wait?" Cody said, reaching out to touch her face. "Promise? There's something I've got to ask you."

Nodding, Maggy turned and walked off the stage with Bobby in her arms. She pressed her face close to Bobby's. "I love you, too, Sport," she whispered softly.

"Love Ma-ma," Bobby repeated, winding his chubby arms around her neck and clinging tightly.

It was at least half an hour before Cody was free. He had abandoned his suit jacket, and his tie was hanging loose around his neck. Maggy was certain she'd never seen him look more wonderful.

He didn't say a word. He just walked up to her and hauled them both into his arms.

"Oh, Mags," he whispered softly, his voice filled with emotion. "I planned to come back after the ceremony. But I wanted you to have some time to think. I didn't want you to make any hasty decisions about your job. I didn't want you to do anything you might regret. That's where I was all day yesterday. I came in and talked to Alice Spenser, the editor of *Modern Motherhood*. I told her the whole story."

"But what about Priscilla?"

"Priscilla who?" he murmured, nuzzling her neck.

"Priscilla the prissy blonde. You know, the one you hired to accept the award for you."

Cody leaned back and grinned wickedly. "I lied."

"You what!"

"Lied," he said, covering her mouth with a quick kiss. "I knew I had to tell you something, didn't I?" Cody looked deep into her eyes. "I just didn't want you to do anything you'd regret, honey."

"The only thing I regret," she said tenderly, sliding her hand across his cheek, "is that it took me so long to realize just what was important to me." Maggy pulled out of his arms. "There's something else we have to discuss. Bobby and I had a long talk, and he's agreed to marry me." She grinned as Cody's brows rose.

"He did, did he?" Cody said in amusement.

"But the problem is, he's a little worried. Bobby says you and he come as a package deal, and that if I marry him, you've got to come along too. So—what do you think?"

Cody grinned mischievously. "Seems to me you're getting a deal. Two men for the price of one."

"Does that mean yes?" she asked breathlessly, her eyes on his.

"What about your job?" Cody inquired hesitantly, a dark shadow filling his eyes. Maggy wound her arms around his neck. "I don't want you to do anything that—"

"What job?" she murmured, pressing her lips to his.

"You didn't, did you?" Cody drew back to look at her, a stunned look of surprise on his face.

"I sure did. I resigned. Cody, I told you last night, I can always get another job."

Cody threw back his head and laughed. "Do you realize that between the two of us—" he glanced at

Bobby "—well, the three of us, we don't have one job between us. Once my editors at Adventure find out I went ahead and accepted this award, I doubt if I'll be writing for them anymore."

"So?" Maggy queried saucily. "I'm not worried. I'm sure something will work out."

Cody nuzzled her neck. "You do realize that quitting your job wasn't sensible, reasonable or—"

"Rational," she supplied huskily, leaning closer to Cody. "And you never answered my question. Are you going to marry me, or not?"

"I am," he assured her, bending to cover her lips with his. "I certainly am, especially since you beat me to the punch with that question by almost ten seconds." He flashed her a wink as he hauled her into his arms once more.

"Face it, Mags, it's the only *sensible* thing to do."

Epilogue

"Children, it was a lovely ceremony." Elizabeth dabbed at her eyes and kissed Cody and Maggy on the cheek. They were standing in the vestibule of the church, waiting to greet their guests for the first time as Mr. and Mrs. William Cody. And family. "I cried through the whole thing." Sniffling, Elizabeth looked lovingly at Maggy. "And you, dear, you made a beautiful bride." Her eyes went over Maggy's wedding dress. It was antique satin and lace with leg-o'-mutton sleeves and a long, flowing train. "I've never seen you look lovelier."

"Thank you, Mother," Maggy whispered, kissing her mother's cheek. "You look wonderful, too." Maggy's gaze traveled over her mother. For once in her life, her mother had surprised her. Her floor-length silk dress in the palest shade of peach was intricately patterned with beading. A matching pill-box hat with plumes of the same shade of peach sat atop her head. In her ears she wore diamond earrings—that matched. She looked wonderful, too wonderful.

"Mother," Maggy said worriedly. "What do you have on your feet?"

"My feet, dear?" Elizabeth inched backward a fraction.

"Yes, Mother," Maggy said, trying not to smile. "Your feet. Let me see them."

"Well, children, I'd better join Chester in the receiving line. Here, give me Bobby," Elizabeth said, plucking the tuxedo-clad toddler from Cody's arms. "See you later." Elizabeth darted away.

"Mother!" Maggy hissed, craning her neck to see. "I'll bet she's wearing those neon-green glow-in-the-dark tennis shoes," she muttered, turning to Cody.

"Come on now, Mags, stop scowling. Here comes the photographer. You want him to think you're looking like that because you're sorry you married me?" Cody gazed at her, a twinkle in his eye.

"Mr. and Mrs. Cody, look this way, please?"

Maggy and Cody turned, smiling brightly. "Mags?" Cody whispered. "How do you feel about Seattle?"

"Is this a trick question?" Maggy asked, wondering what her feelings about Seattle had to do with what was going on at the moment.

"No, no, no," Cody assured her, placing his hand on her elbow and guiding her in the direction the photographer was indicating. "I was just wondering how you felt about Seattle."

"Well, I've never been there." She glanced suspiciously at her husband. "Why all this interest in Seattle all of a sudden? I thought we were going to Hawaii for our honeymoon."

"Mrs. Cody, please?" The photographer sighed. "Could I have your attention for just a few moments?"

"Behave yourself," Cody admonished, trying to hold back a grin.

"Cody?" she whispered out of the side of her mouth, mindful of the photographer who was watching her intently. "What's going on?"

"Now promise you're not going to get upset?"

Oh Lord! She recognized that tone of voice!

"I promise I'm not going to get upset," Maggy assured him, trying not to smile at the devilish look on his face.

"Well, Mags, have you ever heard of a romance novel called *Love's Sweet Honor*?"

"Heard of it?" Forgetting the photographer, Maggy whipped her head around. "Cody, that's the book that caused so much trouble for Rebecca English. Remember I told you she got caught reading it in cla—'' The mischievous look on Cody's face made Maggy stop abruptly. "Why do you want to know if I've ever heard of—? Oh no!" Maggy's eyes grew round with surprise. "Cody," she moaned. "Tell me you didn't!"

His grin widened.

"Oh Lord," she said glumly. "You did, didn't you? You wrote *Love's Sweet Honor*."

Cody nodded his head slowly. Here we go again, Maggy thought in amusement.

"So—what does *Love's Sweet Honor* have to do with Seattle?" Why did she have the feeling she was going to be sorry she asked? Perhaps it was the devilish look on her husband's face.

"Well," he said slowly, his mouth curving upward. "*Love's Sweet Honor* is a finalist in a contest for Best Romance Novel of the year. And the award ceremony is in—"

"Seattle," she finished for him, suddenly putting all the pieces together. Maggy sighed. "When do we leave?"

Cody glanced at his watch. "In about forty minutes, and if we don't hurry, we're going to miss our plane."

"Forty minutes!" Maggy cried in alarm. "Cody, I can't get on a plane in a wedding dress! And what about Bobby?"

"Mrs. Cody, please?" The photographer stood up

and sighed heavily. "If you'll just give me your attention for a few more moments, please? I promise I'll try to hurry."

"Now Mags," Cody said gently. "You promised you weren't going to get upset. Now don't worry about your clothes. Your mother brought your suitcases and a change; they're already waiting in the limo. And Bobby and your mother are meeting us in Seattle next week. So—what do you think?" He grinned down at her, and Maggy smiled.

"I think you had this all planned."

"I did," Cody confirmed, bending to brush his lips across hers. "After all, everyone knows I'm a very reasonable, rational, sensible person."

"I wouldn't bet the farm on that," she cautioned with a laugh.

"We don't own a farm," Cody pointed out. "I love you, Mags," he said softly, bending down to scoop Maggy up into his arms.

"I love you, too," Maggy whispered, as Cody's lips found hers.

"Hold that pose!" the photographer cried, snapping away.

"Cody," Maggy murmured, laying her head on her husband's shoulder as he started toward the door. "Now I know how you got your nickname."

"That's not why, honey." Laughing softly, Cody pushed open the church door, then came to a halt as he bent to kiss her lips again. "Mags, honey," he whispered, his eyes shining with love. "As soon as we get to Seattle, I promise to show you just *how* I got my nickname." He wiggled his brows suggestively, and Maggy laughed softly.

"Is this the fun part?" she whispered and Cody threw back his head and laughed again as he started down the steps.

"Mags, honey, this is *definitely* the fun part."

* * * * *

SILHOUETTE *Romance*

Escape to a place where a kiss is still a kiss...
Feel the breathless connection...
Fall in love as though it were
the very first time...
Experience the power of love!

Come to where favorite authors—such as
Diana Palmer, Stella Bagwell,
Marie Ferrarella and many more—
deliver heart-warming romance and genuine
emotion, time after time after time....

Silhouette Romance—
stories straight from the heart!

Silhouette®
Where love comes alive™

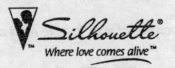

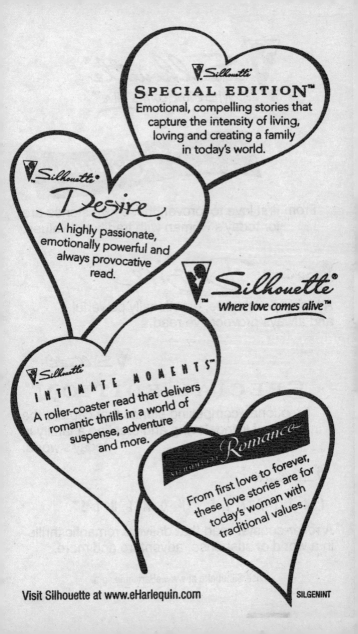

Where love comes alive™

From first love to forever, these love stories are
for today's woman with traditional values.

 Desire

A highly passionate, emotionally powerful
and always provocative read.

Silhouette®

SPECIAL EDITION™

Emotional, compelling stories that capture the
intensity of living, loving and creating a family in
today's world.

Silhouette®

INTIMATE MOMENTS™

A roller-coaster read that delivers romantic thrills
in a world of suspense, adventure and more.

Visit Silhouette at www.eHarlequin.com

SDIR2

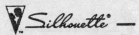

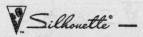